DOCTOR · WHO

Forever Autumn

DOCTOR·WHO

Forever
Autumn

MARK MORRIS

BOOKS

2 4 6 8 10 9 7 5 3 1

Published in 2007 by BBC Books, an imprint of Ebury Publishing.
Ebury Publishing is a division of the Random House Group Ltd.

© Mark Morris, 2007

Mark Morris has asserted his right to be identified as the author of this
Work in accordance with the Copyright, Design and Patents Act 1988.

Doctor Who is a BBC Wales production for BBC One
Executive Producers: Russell T Davies and Julie Gardner
Series Producer: Phil Collinson

Original series broadcast on BBC Television. Format © BBC 1963.
'Doctor Who', 'TARDIS' and the Doctor Who logo are trademarks of the
British Broadcasting Corporation and are used under licence.

The Random House Group Ltd Reg. No. 954009.
Addresses for companies within the Random House Group can be found
at www.randomhouse.co.uk.

A CIP catalogue record for this book is available from the British Library.

ISBN 978 1 84607 270 3

The Random House Group Ltd makes every effort to ensure that the
papers used in our books are made from trees that have been legally
sourced from well-managed credibly certified forests. Our paper
procurement policy can be found at www.randomhouse.co.uk.

Series Consultant: Justin Richards
Project Editor: Steve Tribe
Cover design by Lee Binding © BBC 2007

Typeset in Albertina and Deviant Strain
Printed and bound in Germany by GGP Media GmbH, Poessneck

For David and Polly,
who share that Saturday feeling.

A Doctor to call your own.

When the bell finally rang, Rick Pirelli almost burst with excitement. Now there was nothing standing between him and the monsters.

He spotted his best friends, Scott Beaumont and Thad Steiner, in the school yard. From a distance his buddies always reminded him of Laurel and Hardy, one tall and wide, the other short and skinny. He ran up to them, swinging his bag around his head in sheer exhilaration. 'Hey, you guys!'

They turned to him. Scott, who played quarter-back in the school under-13s football team, had a wide grin on his chubby, red face.

'Ricky baby,' he boomed. 'How's it going?'

Rick thumped to a stop. The cool air felt great on his hot skin. 'Man, I thought today was going to go on *forever*,' he said.

'Yeah, me too,' said Scott. 'It was like we were stuck in a time zone or something.'

'Warp,' said Thad quietly.

'Huh?'

'It's time *warp*, not time *zone*. A time *zone* is just like whatever time it is in whichever part of the world you're in. There are twenty-four time zones on the planet. But a time *warp* is like a time distortion, so it seems as if—'

Scott rolled his eyes at Rick, who grinned back at him. 'Yeah, Thad, what*ever*,' he said.

They set off home, Rick – medium build, tousled chestnut hair, a 'cute nose' according to Beverley Masterson, who sat behind him in Math – strolling between his two friends. Scott, on his right, seemed almost to bounce as he walked. For a big guy he was full of energy, and deceptively athletic. Thad, by contrast, was like a mouse, a little blond mouse with specs, which were constantly slipping down his nose. He was studious and precise and he read truck-loads of books, mainly science fiction, but all kinds of other stuff too. Maybe for that reason he told the best stories – at camp it was always Thad's ghost stories the other guys wanted to hear. He could also be side-splittingly funny, though half the time he didn't even seem to realise he *was* being funny, and in a way that made him funnier still.

Rick was feeling good – great, in fact. It was Friday afternoon, school was out, and tomorrow was Halloween, which meant all the usual fun stuff – dressing up, trick-or-treating, bobbing for apples, eating candy. Then later, when it was dark, he and his friends would head down to the Halloween Carnival, which was always a big deal in Blackwood Falls, where they would eat as many hot dogs and go on as many rides as possible, and watch the ceremonial burning of the Pumpkin Man. And then, later *still* – if Scott hadn't thrown up and gone home, like he did last year – they would head back to Rick's and spend what was left of the night watching scary movies in their sleeping bags until they fell asleep.

Could life *get* any better, he thought. As the three of them tromped through the quiet, tree-lined streets, Scott yakking about some old movie he'd seen on cable the night before, something about a guy who shrank to the size of an ant and had a fight with a giant spider, Rick looked around, taking in the sights, drinking it all in. It seemed to him that *everyone* in Blackwood Falls loved Halloween. Maybe, he thought, the Mayor or the town committee or whatever wouldn't let you live here if you didn't. Wherever he looked, front porches were bedecked with Halloween pumpkins, trees were hung with rubber spiders and bats, and windows were festooned with spray-on cobwebs, paper skeletons, cardboard witches and leering rubber masks.

The air even *smelled* right, of dry leaves and wood smoke and damp, mulchy earth.

This was gonna be the best Halloween *ever*, he thought.

Rick's house was one of the biggest and oldest in Blackwood Falls, a sprawling colonial residence surrounded by a picket fence, flanked by well-established trees and fronted by a long porch. When the boys were hanging out, it was where they usually ended up, mainly because it was the closest of all their houses to the school, and also to the town's main square, which – once they'd dumped their stuff and grabbed a snack – was where they were imminently headed.

They clattered through the front door, dropping bags as they went, and into the kitchen.

'Hi, Mom!' Rick shouted.

'Hi, honey!' came a voice from upstairs. Half a minute later, Mrs Pirelli appeared. She was a willowy, dark-haired woman, with a nose even cuter than Rick's.

'You boys doing OK?' she asked.

'Sure,' replied Scott, his mouth stuffed with an almost entire Hershey bar.

'Yes, thank you, Mrs Pirelli,' said Thad.

She smiled at them. 'Betcha can't wait till tomorrow. You picking up your costumes today?'

'Yep, Mom, right after this,' said Rick.

'You all got your money to pay Mr Tozier?'

They nodded.

'OK, well here's an extra ten dollars to buy yourselves some ice cream afterward. If you like, I'll run you guys home later.'

'Wow, thanks, Mrs Pirelli,' said Scott, his enthusiasm drowning out Thad's grateful murmuring.

'Yeah, thanks, Mom,' said Rick.

Her smile widened. 'My pleasure. Have fun, guys. I'll leave you to it.' She exited the room with a little wave.

'Your mom is *so* cool!' said Scott.

'You've just got the hots for her,' Rick teased.

Scott's face turned an even deeper crimson than usual. 'Have not!'

'How come you're blushing then?'

'I'm not!'

'Are so.'

'Hey, guys,' Thad said quietly, 'look at this.'

He was standing in front of the big window over the sink that looked out over the long back garden.

'What is it?' asked Scott, glad of the distraction.

'It's the tree. There's something weird about it.'

Rick and Scott joined Thad at the window. At

the bottom of the garden, in front of the high fence that separated their property from that of old Mrs Helligan, was the most famous tree in Blackwood Falls. It was, in fact, the tree which had given the town its name – although, oddly, no one seemed to know what *kind* of tree it was. All Rick knew was that its gnarled trunk was as black as charcoal, and that it was ugly and twisted and had never, as long as he'd been alive, sprouted either buds or leaves. He wasn't sure whether the tree was *actually* dead, but it certainly looked as though it was. It looked like it had been killed by a disease or something, because its branches were covered in lumpy black growths, like boils or tumours. When he'd been a little kid, Rick had thought the growths were the tree's eyes, watching him.

'I don't see anything weird,' Scott said now.

'There was a green light,' said Thad. 'Like phosphorescence.'

'Phosphor-what?'

'It's a light produced during a chemical reaction, like when fungus is rotting.'

Scott sniffed. 'So the tree's covered in rotting fungus? Big deal.'

'No, but this was different. Strange. *There, look!*'

All three of them saw it this time, a peculiar green glimmer that seemed to flash up from the dark earth at the base of the trunk.

'Freaky,' said Scott.

Thad turned, his pale blue eyes wide behind his spectacles. 'Let's investigate.'

They went outside. Rick had never liked the tree. As a kid he'd been scared of it, and now that he was older he kept away from it for fear of catching something from its raddled bark. Even his parents gave the thing a wide berth. The soil down that end of the garden had always been crummy anyway, so they had no reason to go near it. The closest any of them ever got was when his dad mowed the lawn.

Standing at the base of the tree now, Rick realised it was the nearest he'd come to it in years. Maybe ever.

'There's nothing here now,' he said.

'Not even any fungus,' said Scott gloomily.

'Maybe whatever made the light is underground,' suggested Thad.

Rick pulled a face. 'How can it be?'

'I dunno, but maybe it is.'

'Hey, maybe it's buried treasure,' said Scott. 'Emeralds or something. Maybe we should dig down, see if we can find anything.'

'Aw, c'mon guys,' said Rick. 'This is a waste of time. Let's go pick up our costumes.'

'Don't be a wienie,' said Scott.

'Couldn't we just dig down a little way?' said Thad.

Rick sighed. 'OK, if it'll make you lame-brains happy. But I'm telling you, it's pointless.'

He trudged back to the house. It had been raining on and off for the past week and the ground was a little squelchy underfoot. He reappeared a minute later with his dad's spade from the garage, which he handed to Thad.

'You wanna dig, you dig,' he said.

Thad took the spade and used it to prod at the ground. Scott rolled his eyes.

'What're you doing? Tickling the worms? Give it to me.'

Thad handed the spade over without protest and Scott began to hack at the clay-like earth. Within a couple of minutes sweat was rolling down his face, but he had managed to create a sizeable hole.

Suddenly Thad shouted, 'Hey, stop! I see something!'

'What?' said Rick.

'I dunno. Look there.' Thad pointed into the hole, and all at once what little colour he had seemed to drain from his face. 'Aw, jeez, you don't think it's a body, do you?'

All three peered into the hole. There *was* something down there. Something brownish and leathery and smooth. Was it skin, wondered Rick. Dry-mouthed, he took the spade from Scott's slack hand and began to probe tentatively into the hole, loosening thick clots of earth from around the object. He uncovered an edge, a corner. Suddenly he relaxed.

'It's not a body,' he said. 'I think it's an old book.'

He lowered himself to his knees in the mud and leaned into the hole. There was an unpleasant smell, like mouldy bread or rotting vegetables. Holding his breath, he leaned in further, grabbed the leathery object and tried to tug it from the earth. He half-expected it to disintegrate in his hands, but it came free with a thick *schlup* sound.

The book was big, like an old Bible, and its cover was made of a weird brownish-red substance that was a bit like leather and a bit like plastic, and also, thought Rick with distaste, a bit like flesh. He straightened up and his friends crowded round to look.

'Cool,' muttered Thad.

'Awesome,' breathed Scott.

Rick produced a handkerchief and wiped away as much of the muck as he could. Emblazoned on the book's cover, or rather carved into it, was a strange oval symbol criss-crossed with jagged lines. When Rick tilted the book, the symbol seemed to flash momentarily with a peculiar green light.

'Did you see that?' said Scott.

'Reflection, that's all,' Rick mumbled.

There was nothing else on the book's cover, nor on the spine. Nothing but the oval symbol. For some reason the book creeped Rick out a little. Holding it gave him a shivery feeling, as if he was holding a box full of snakes. Almost reluctantly he opened the book at random, tilting his head back as if he expected something to jump out at him. The thick, wrinkly pages were covered in what he at first thought were random shapes, unfamiliar symbols. Then, just for a second, he felt dizzy, and all at once his eyes seemed to adjust. And he realised that the shapes were not shapes at all, but letters; letters which formed words. He tried to read the words, but they seemed jumbled up, foreign maybe. What was more they gave him the kind of prickly feeling you get when you think someone is standing behind you in an empty room.

'Esoterica,' said Thad.

'Who?' said Scott.

'Like a secret language, known only to a small number of people.'

'Is that what that is?' asked Scott.

Thad shrugged. 'That's what it looks like.'

'Hey,' said Scott, 'maybe this book belonged to, like, devil worshippers, and maybe these words are spells to call up demons or something.'

'Could be,' said Thad.

'So why don't we try it? See what happens?'

Rick slammed the book shut. 'No.'

'Aw, c'mon, man,' said Scott, screwing up his face, 'don't be such a *girl*. What's the worst that can happen?'

How could Rick explain the effect the book was having on him without making it sound dumb? Maybe if his friends actually *held* the book in their hands…

'Here you go,' he said, thrusting it at Scott, 'if you wanna call up a demon, you call up a demon. But don't blame me if it bites your stupid head off.'

Scott rolled his eyes and took the book. Rick expected to see a change come over him, a look of unease appear on his face. But Scott just opened the book and started to read from it.

'Belloris,' he said, 'Crakithe, Meladran, Sandreath, Pellorium, Canitch, Leemanec, Freegor, Maish…'

The weird thing, the really *creepy* thing, was that Scott seemed to have no trouble reading the arcane words. He read them in a strong, confident voice, almost as if he was doing a roll-call of his classmates' names or reading out a list of the American states. Another weird thing was that almost as soon as he started to read his eyes went glassy and his body went rigid. Watching him, Rick couldn't help thinking that the book had him under some kind of spell and, somehow or other, was bringing the words to life *through* him.

But that was nuts.

Wasn't it?

'OK,' he said, trying to make it sound as if he was bored, 'you can stop now.'

But Scott carried on as if he hadn't heard: 'Mullarkiss, Sothor, Lantrac, Ithe…'

'I said *stop!*' yelled Rick, and snatched the book from his hands. This time when he slammed it shut sparkles of green light seemed to puff up from the pages like dust. Rick blinked to clear his vision. Man, why was he getting so worked up?

Scott swayed a moment, blinking rapidly. He looked like someone coming out of a trance.

'You OK?' asked Thad.

Scott scowled. 'Sure I am. Why shouldn't I be?'

'You turned really freaky for a minute there.'

'And you should know,' said Scott, sounding like his old self, 'being Mr Freaky 24-7.'

They trudged back to the house, Rick carrying the book. He was wondering what to do with it, wondering whether he should show it to his parents. But when his dad appeared at the back door he found himself instinctively shoving it behind his back.

'What have you reprobates been up to?' Mr Pirelli asked good-humouredly. He was tall, a little thin on top, but he had kind of a goofy grin, which made him look younger than he was.

'Nothing, Mr Pirelli,' said Thad quickly.

'Dad,' Rick said. 'Why aren't you at work?'

'I brought some stuff home to do on computer. It's easier to concentrate here.' Tony Pirelli noticed the state of his son's clothes. 'Heck, Rick, what have you been doing? Rolling in the dirt?'

Before Rick could come up with a convincing explanation, Scott blurted, 'We've been digging for treasure, Mr Pirelli. Under the old tree.'

Tony Pirelli unveiled his goofy grin. 'That so? You find anything?'

'Yeah, a big fat zero,' said Rick before his friends could reply.

'Pity. Well, you guys take your shoes off before you come inside. And Rick, get yourself cleaned up. Your mom would have kittens if she found out you'd gone to town looking like a vagrant.'

The walls of Rick's room were covered in movie posters – *Lord of the Rings*, *X-Men*, *Ghost Rider*, James Bond. He had a computer and a TV and his shelves were stacked with books, comics, games and plastic models of dinosaurs, robots and spaceships. It was a typical 12-year-old's room, in other words.

He pushed the book under the bed, glad to relieve himself of its fleshy clamminess. He was standing in his boxers, rooting through his drawers for his favourite T-shirt and jeans, when there came a tap-tap-tap on his door.

Thad was sitting on the bed, flicking through a *Spider-Man* comic; Scott was swinging himself back and forth on the swivel chair in front of Rick's desk. All three boys looked at each other, a moment of unspoken tension passing between them.

Then Rick called, 'Who is it?'

Silence.

He licked his lips, called again, and when no one answered a second time he said casually, 'Grab that, would you, Thad?'

For a moment he thought Thad would refuse, but then he shrugged and said, 'Sure.'

He crossed the room and pulled the door open. The landing outside was deserted.

'There's no one—' Thad started to say – and then a figure with a brown, rotting face and long pointed teeth leaped into the room, screeching.

Thad dived onto the bed, Scott screamed and propelled himself backwards in the swivel chair, crashing into the desk, and Rick held his T-shirt up in front of him like a flimsy shield.

The brown-faced monstrosity started to laugh. It doubled over, slapping its thighs. Then it peeled off its face to reveal a more human one underneath

– that of Rick's 16-year-old brother, and bane of his life, Chris.

'You should see yourselves,' Chris hooted. 'Man, what a bunch o' pansies.'

'Get lost, Chris,' muttered Rick, but Chris stood there, relishing his victory.

'Literally scared the pants off yer, didn't I?' he said, and hooted again.

'Yeah, yeah, whatever,' said Rick. 'Now go away, will you? And put the mask back on. You're too ugly without it.'

Chris made an L-sign on his forehead with his thumb and forefinger. 'So long, losers,' he said, heading out of the room.

'Man, your brother is such a dweeb,' Scott told Rick after the door had closed.

Finding the book, and their encounter with Chris, had soured Rick's mood. For a moment he felt like snapping that he'd call Chris back so Scott could tell him that to his face, but he forced himself to swallow the words. 'Forget about him,' he said, pulling on his T-shirt and jeans. By the time he had tied his sneakers he was feeling a little better.

'Come on,' he said, 'let's go get our costumes.'

'And our ice creams,' Scott reminded him, licking his lips. 'Triple chocolate sundae, here I come.'

* * *

Etta Helligan, known to local children as the Witch Lady, knew that something was wrong. She knew it as surely as day followed night, and night followed day. She knew it because she could feel it in her bones and her guts – an ache, a tingle, a sense of dread. A key had been turned, a door had been opened, and something… something *bad*, something *terrible*, had stepped out of the darkness and into the world.

'What is it, Romeo?' she murmured to the black cat crouched on the topmost stair, staring at her with yellow eyes. 'What do you see?'

The cat miaowed and coiled itself round her ankles as Etta reached the upper landing. She bent to scratch its head absently, then plodded on through to her room.

There were more cats in here, Orlando sprawled on the bed, Marmalade prowling along the top of the wardrobe. Etta crossed to the window, noting how the clouds were bunching in the sky like grey fists, blotting the light from the land. She peered out, not knowing what she was looking for – and that was when she saw it.

Of course. How foolish of her not to have realised. Now that she could see the tree, black and twisted, clawing at the sky, it seemed obvious that it was the focus of her disquiet. She didn't know *how* she knew, she just did. She had spent a lifetime *just knowing* things, and she had become used to it. Her mother had been the same, and *her* mother before her.

When she'd been younger, Etta had tried to help people by warning them about things, usually bad things, that she *just knew* were going to happen. But nobody ever thanked her for her advice. On the contrary, more often than not, they reacted angrily, thinking she was somehow responsible for the terrible events she foresaw. And as the years passed, and word got around, people started to shun her, believing she was a bad omen, a jonah. Believing that disaster clung to her like a contagion, waiting to be passed on.

Well then, she had thought finally, if they didn't want her help, so be it. And so for the past forty years or more she had all but withdrawn from the life of the town. For Etta it was too painful to see someone walking on the sidewalk or out buying groceries and to know that they were in for a fall, yet not be able to do a thing about it.

But this was different. This, she felt sure, was something that would affect not just one person or one family, but the whole population of the Falls. She didn't know what the *something* was yet, but she knew it meant them harm.

But how to proceed? How to warn her fellow townsfolk? She didn't know that, but she *did* know she had to do *something*. This time she couldn't simply bury her head in the sand.

She stared at the black tree, willing it to give up its secrets. And suddenly, as though complying with her request, she saw something drift from the tree's base and curl around its trunk. Was it smoke? No, it was more like mist. A greenish mist, rising out of the ground. As Etta watched, the mist thickened and began to spread, extending wispy tendrils which crept outwards in all directions. Soon the tree was little more than a black haze in the greenish gloom.

ONE

The Doctor catapulted from the TARDIS, sonic screwdriver held out in front of him. He pivoted on his heels, turning a full circle. 'Come on, come on,' he muttered.

Martha stepped out of the TARDIS behind him, a look of gleeful expectation on her face. When she saw she was in a backyard between a couple of smelly bins, rather than on some alien planet with pink skies and purple grass, she frowned.

'Is this where the signal was coming from?' she asked.

'It wasn't a signal,' he said absently, 'more a sort of… splurge. A big fat splurge of power.'

'But what kind of power? I mean, what made it so special?'

'It was old,' he said, still not looking at her.

'How old?'

'Oh… very, very, very, very, very, *very* old, I'd say. Old enough to make my teeth itch. And my palms.' He examined the palm of his left hand thoughtfully. 'Maybe I'm allergic.'

'You'd better avoid Keith Richards then,' said Martha. 'He'd bring you out in hives.'

The sonic screwdriver didn't bleep or shine brighter or anything, but suddenly the Doctor shouted, 'You beauty! Go on, girl!' Next second, he was running towards a gate in the high fence surrounding the yard, all bony knees and elbows, his spiky, tousled hair seeming to fizz with energy.

Martha ran after him. She both loved and hated it when he was like this. She found it exhilarating and frustrating at the same time. He was a bit like a brilliant but temperamental racehorse. Sometimes all you could do was hang on for dear life and hope you wouldn't fall off and be left on the track, coughing and spluttering in his wake.

'So where are we?' she shouted as he yanked back the bolts on the gate and threw it open.

'Somewhere in New England,' he called over his shoulder.

'Is that New England on New Earth or New England in old America?'

'The second one,' he said.

They followed whatever signals the Doctor was getting from the sonic for maybe fifteen minutes. To Martha's relief they didn't run the whole time. The Doctor alternated his pace between sprinting, jogging and strolling, depending on the strength or accuracy of the signal. A few times he stopped completely and cast about in a circle; on one occasion he even pointed the sonic straight up at the darkening sky before shaking his head.

During their search, Martha looked around as much as she was able, drinking in her surroundings. It turned out they had landed behind an ice cream parlour called Harry Ho's, which was one of numerous stores and eating places fringing the main, tree-lined square of a small, picturesque town called Blackwood Falls. She got the name of the place from a big banner strung across the main street advertising the Blackwood Falls Halloween Carnival. Even without the banner she would have guessed the time of year, simply from the profusion of window displays featuring carved pumpkins, witches, ghosts, skeletons and the like. She thought the green mist which began to envelop them as they moved out from the town centre and into the suburbs was taking things a bit too far, though. The mist was odourless but chilly. It felt like someone caressing her cheeks with cold fingers.

'Doctor, what is this stuff?' she asked.

He shrugged. He'd slowed to a walking pace now, which he seemed, for the moment, content to maintain. 'One thing it's *not* is of this earth.'

'It's alien, you mean?' She linked her arm with his. She didn't want him to bolt off again and lose her in the fog. 'Is it sentient?'

'Nah. It's just a by-product of the energy…'

'Splurge?'

He grinned. 'That, yeah.'

'It's not toxic, is it?'

'Don't think so. Least I'm not picking up anything.'

Three minutes later he stopped outside the gate of what appeared to be a big clapboard house with a long front porch. It was hard to tell because the mist seemed to be at its thickest here, reducing the building to a dark blocky haze.

'It's here,' he said.

'In the house?'

'Behind it. Come on.' He vaulted the fence and ran across the lawn and up the side of the house, Martha in tow. She felt a tingle of excitement, wondering what marvels were in store for her this time.

'A dead tree?' she said. 'Is that it?'

The Doctor prowled around the base of the tree, his hands in his trouser pockets. He produced a pair of black-rimmed spectacles and slipped them on, then bent over to peer at something. 'Ooh, look,' he said, 'a hole.'

Martha stood beside him, wrinkling her nose. The mist might not smell of anything, but the tree, or something close to it, did. It was the smell of something dead.

'A burrow?' she ventured.

'I'd say it's more likely someone's been digging,' said the Doctor. 'Look how smooth the sides are. I wonder what they found.'

'You think something old and alien was lying dormant under here, and that when it was dug up, it came alive and sent out that… power splurge?'

The Doctor gave her one of his heart-melting grins. 'That's what I love about you, Martha Jones!' he cried. 'You use your brain!'

Martha tried not to look flattered. She watched as the Doctor examined one of the black warty growths that covered the tree. He put his face up so close to it she expected him to sniff it, or maybe even give it a lick. Instead he whipped out his trusty sonic again, pointed it at the growth and turned it on.

The result was spectacular. The growth, plus another dozen or so close to it, unfurled and launched itself from the tree. All at once Martha found herself fighting off squealing, fist-sized creatures, which appeared to be composed of a spindly, thrashing tangle of black roots. She felt them scratching her hands and scuttling lopsidedly up the sleeves of her jacket to reach her face. Repulsed, she batted and clawed at them, but each time she managed to fling one away, it propelled itself back into the fray.

Beside her, the Doctor was fighting a similar battle. He tried zapping the creatures with his sonic, but that only seemed to enrage them. Martha became vaguely aware that he was fighting off the rooty things with one hand whilst scrabbling in a jacket pocket with the other. It wasn't until she saw a jet of flame, however, that she allowed herself to glance across at what he was doing.

He had taken a candle from his coat pocket and somehow turned it into a mini-flamethrower with the aid of his sonic screwdriver. He was sweeping it in an arc in front of him now – and it was working! Terrified of the fire, the root-creatures were retreating, scuttling back to the tree and burrowing into the soft earth at its base, like baby chicks seeking security beneath the soft, warm body of their mother.

Within thirty seconds the last of the creatures had disappeared. Martha stood on shaky legs, breathing heavily, trying to rid her mind of the scratchy, crawly feel of their bodies on her skin.

'Well,' said the Doctor conversationally, 'that was unexpected.'

Martha gave one last almighty shudder. 'What *were* those things?'

'Some kind of defence system, I'd say, protecting the big mamma here.'

He blew out the candle. Martha gave him a wry look. 'I can't believe the amount of stuff you've got in your pockets.'

He flipped the candle over his shoulder, caught it neatly behind his back without looking and slipped it back into his pocket. 'Left over from a Barry Manilow concert. Madison Square Garden, 1990. Great gig.' He began to warble the opening bars of *Mandy*.

'Don't do that,' said Martha quickly.

The Doctor gave a wistful smile. 'Brings a tear to your eye, does it?'

'Yeah, but not in a good way.'

'Hey,' a voice called behind them, 'do you mind telling me what you're doing on my property?'

The Doctor and Martha turned to see a tall man striding towards them through the green mist. He looked, thought Martha, like a nice, ordinary bloke, albeit a bit disgruntled.

'We're trespassing,' said the Doctor cheerfully.

The man looked taken aback. 'OK,' he said

slowly, 'well, do you mind telling me *why* you're trespassing?'

The Doctor flashed a look at Martha. 'Ah. Actually we're not trespassing, we're...' he produced his psychic paper and held it up in front of the man's face '... whatever it says here.'

The man took the psychic paper and peered at it. 'Environmental Health and Safety Operative,' he murmured.

'Yep,' said the Doctor, 'that's me.' He leaned forward and suddenly seemed to become very serious. 'Are you aware, Mr...?'

'Pirelli.'

'Are you aware, Mr Pirelli, that you possess a very dangerous tree?'

The man looked up at the tree uncertainly. 'Dangerous?'

'Lethal,' said Martha.

The man licked his lips. 'In what way?'

The Doctor put a reassuring hand on Mr Pirelli's shoulder. Instead of answering his question he said, 'Tell me, Mr Pirelli, has anyone, to your knowledge, dug anything up here recently?'

'Well... my son and his friends were digging here earlier. They said they were looking for buried treasure. You know how boys are.'

'And where's your son now, Mr Pirelli?' the Doctor

asked, his gaze intense, his eyes appearing almost black.

'Um… they headed into town, to get their costumes for tomorrow night. Tozier's Costume Emporium.'

Martha thought the Doctor's next question would be to ask where that was, but he surprised her by saying, 'Across from Harry Ho's ice cream place? Big clown in the window?'

Mr Pirelli nodded.

'Cheers, Mr P. Come on, Martha.' The Doctor began to stride away.

Martha gave the bemused man a sympathetic smile and followed the Doctor.

'My son's not in trouble, is he?' Mr Pirelli called after her.

Crossing her fingers, Martha said, 'Don't worry, Mr Pirelli, we'll sort it out. I'm sure everything will be fine.' She was about to break into a jog when something occurred to her. 'What's your son's name, by the way?'

'Rick,' he said.

She caught up with the Doctor on the pavement heading back into town. He was in brooding mode, hands in pockets, head down. He murmured something as she came abreast of him.

'What?' she said.

He stopped, licked a forefinger and held it up as though testing the wind direction. 'Can you feel that?' he asked.

She could. There was a sense of oppressiveness in the atmosphere, like someone pressing down on her shoulders. 'Yes,' she said, 'but what is it?'

He looked into her eyes. His face was set and serious. So quietly that it made her shiver, he muttered, 'By the pricking of my thumbs, something wicked this way comes...'

TWO

Rick was a werewolf, Scott was Frankenstein's monster and Thad was some sort of cross between a mummy and a ghoul. Or at least, that was what they were going to be tomorrow. Having tried his costume on in the shop, Rick could now hardly wait for the Halloween Carnival. His sour mood of an hour before had evaporated, and he was back to laughing and joking with his friends.

They were crossing the town square to Harry Ho's, each of them carrying a bulging plastic bag emblazoned with the logo for Tozier's Costume Emporium, when Scott elbowed Rick in the ribs.

'Hey, look out, guys,' he muttered, 'here comes old C-C-C-Clayton.'

Rick looked up. Staggering towards them was an old man in a rumpled, food-stained suit and a grubby shirt. His grey hair was sticking up in knotty tufts on one side, as if he'd slept on it, and his sagging jowls were rough with several days' growth of white stubble. His eyes were red-rimmed and bloodshot, his nose as bulbous and purple as a plum.

'Afternoon, b-b-b-boys,' he called, raising his arm in a clumsy wave.

Scott and Thad both sniggered, but Rick felt an ache of sorrow in his belly. Earl Clayton had once been the town's doctor. According to Mom, Dr Clayton had brought not only Rick into the world, but Rick's dad too. He had been well respected in Blackwood Falls, and Rick himself remembered how kind he'd been when Rick had fallen off his bike six years ago and broken his collar bone. And then there had been the time when Gramma had died – Dr Clayton had visited the old lady every night in the last month of her life, and had even come to the funeral.

Now, though, he was a wreck of a man, and a lot of the local kids saw him as a figure of fun. He'd retired four years ago, and two months later his wife had died unexpectedly, which, according to Rick's dad, had knocked the stuffing out of the old guy. He'd hit the bottle hard, and he now spent most of his time propping up the local bar, or sometimes even sitting on the bench in the town square, sipping whisky from a bottle he kept in a brown paper bag in his jacket pocket. Many people had tried to help him, including Rick's mom and dad, but no one had been able to make him mend his ways.

'You can't stop the man drinking,' Rick's dad had said, 'short of sewing his lips together.'

'He's on a one-way path to destruction,' Rick's mom had said, 'and there ain't no one can do a thing about it.'

'Hey there, Dr Clayton,' Rick called now, kind of hoping that the old guy was too drunk to notice how Scott and Thad were laughing at him.

Earl Clayton came to a swaying halt. He peered at Rick through the late-afternoon gloom, screwing up his rheumy eyes. 'Why, it's y-y-young Rick P-P-Pirelli, isn't it?' he slurred.

'Yes, sir,' said Rick loudly, trying to ignore a fresh outbreak of snickering from his friends.

'My, but you're g-g-g-getting tall,' he said. 'You boys g-going to the C-C-Carnival tomorrow?'

'Yes, sir, we'll be there,' Rick said.

'Well, you b-be sure to have f-f-fun. And don't forget to g-give my regards to your p-p-parents.'

'No, sir, I won't. And thank you, sir.'

The old man gave a clumsy salute, which Scott found so hilarious he had to clap a hand over his mouth to prevent himself hooting with laughter.

'Quit it, you two,' Rick muttered when the old guy was out of earshot. They crossed to Harry Ho's, ordered their ice creams and sodas and sat down. Rick felt bad for Dr Clayton, and so steered the conversation away from him and back to the topic of the week: Halloween.

'Hey, what movies do you guys wanna watch tomorrow?'

'*Saw*,' said Scott without hesitation.

'*Final Destination*,' said Thad.

'There's no way my mom would let us watch either of those, and you know it. Come on, guys, get serious. We don't want everything we choose from the video store to get canned.'

They began to discuss the merits and demerits of certain movies, and were still arguing even after their ice cream bowls and drinks cups were empty. They became so involved in a heated exchange about *Psycho* (Rick pushing for the original, Scott saying he'd rather see the colour remake) that none of them noticed the two strangers until a shadow fell over their table.

They looked up to see a skinny guy in a tight suit grinning down at them. The guy was holding a banana split in one hand and a long-handled spoon in the other. He was shovelling ice cream into his smiling mouth as if he hadn't eaten in days.

'Aren't bananas brilliant!' he said.

The boys just stared at him. Finally Rick said, 'Who are you?'

'I'm the Doctor,' said the man, 'and I bet you're Rick.'

'How did you know that?' Rick asked.

'Well… you look like a Rick. You're all kind of Rick-like. I knew a Rick once. Well, a Ricky. Well, a Mickey really. Except there were two of them. And one of them *was* called Ricky, but I didn't really get to know *him* all that well. Mickey, though… aw, brilliant, he turned out to be. Prince among men. Top banana. Which, funnily enough, brings us back to bananas again. Mind if I sit down?'

The guy had spouted all this at breakneck speed. Rick felt as though he'd been bombarded with words. 'Er… what do you want?' he said.

The Doctor waggled his empty ice cream bowl. 'Another one of these would go down a treat.' He turned and yelled across the room. 'Same again when you've got a minute, Harry! Ta.' Turning to the girl beside him – who, Rick now noticed, was both beautiful and eating something chocolaty with caramel sauce – the Doctor said, 'What about you, Martha? Fancy another?'

'I've barely started this one,' she said.

'Please yourself. Now, where were we? Oh yeah,

we were about to sit down.'

He grabbed a chair from the next table, swung it round and plonked himself into it. Then he jumped up again almost immediately.

'Whoops, manners,' he said, and offered the chair to the girl he'd called Martha. He grabbed another for himself, sat down and leaned forward on his bony elbows, as if he and the boys were about to tell each other their deepest secrets.

'So,' he murmured, 'dug up anything good lately?'

The boys looked at each other in alarm. 'Who did you say you were again?' asked Thad nervously.

'He's the Doctor and I'm Martha,' said the girl, and nodded at Thad and Scott. 'So what do they call you two then?'

They told her. Rick said, 'You say you're the doctor? So do you mean you're, like, the *new* doctor?'

'Interesting question,' said the Doctor reflectively, and tilted himself so far back in his chair he looked in danger of toppling over. 'I suppose that all depends, doesn't it?'

'On what?' asked Scott.

'On when you meet me. I mean, if you meet me in your past and my future, I'd be the new Doctor to you, but the old Doctor to me, whereas if you meet the old me in *your* future, I'd be the new Doctor now and the old Doctor later. You see?'

'Huh?' said Scott.

The Doctor lunged forward again, his chair crashing back down onto all four legs, making Scott jump. Staring at the boy intently, he said, 'You *haven't* met the future me by any chance, have you?'

'Er… no,' whimpered Scott.

'Aw, pity. I wanted to know whether I was ginger.'

Martha cleared her throat. 'I think we're getting off the point,' she said.

'Quite right,' said the Doctor. 'That's Rick, that is, trying to avoid answering the question.'

'What question?' said Rick.

'You were about to tell us what you dug up.'

'Why should we tell *you?*' Scott blurted.

'Because,' said the Doctor quietly, 'if you don't there's a very, *very* strong likelihood that you won't live to see your… how old are you?'

'Twelve,' said Scott.

'OK,' said the Doctor, rotating his fingers in an anti-clockwise direction, '… your thirteenth birthday.'

'Hey!' exclaimed Rick. 'Are you threatening us, mister? 'Cos if you are—'

'Calm down,' Martha said, putting a hand on his arm. Despite his indignation, her touch gave Rick a warm tingly feeling.

'Of course he's not threatening you,' she continued. 'He's trying to warn you. He's trying to save your life.'

'Save my life?' said Rick. 'But… but why does my life *need* saving?'

'Because that thing you dug up – whatever it is – is *dangerous*,' said the Doctor.

'*Very* dangerous,' added Martha.

'Oh, yeah,' the Doctor agreed, 'very, very. And add another great big dollop of very, with lashings of very on top.'

'But… how do you know?' asked Thad.

'I just do,' said the Doctor. 'I'm clever like that.'

'Believe me, guys,' said Martha, 'you're doing yourselves no favours by keeping schtum about this. We're probably the only two people who can help you.'

The boys looked at each other, and her, uncertainly. The Doctor sighed and pointed out of the window. 'That green mist?' he said. 'That's you, that is.'

They looked out of the window, and all three of them gasped. An eerie green mist was creeping into the town square.

'What is it?' whispered Thad.

'It came out of the hole you dug,' said the Doctor. 'Whatever was in there was dormant and now it isn't. It's very old and very deadly.'

Scott looked as though he was about to throw up. 'It was only a book,' he wailed.

'At last,' said the Doctor, 'a chink of daylight. Give that man a pineapple.'

'What sort of book?' Martha asked.

'Dunno,' said Rick. 'It had weird words in it, like a foreign language or something.'

The Doctor's second banana split arrived. He devoured it in three gulps. 'Where's this book now?' he asked, spitting ice cream.

'Under my bed,' said Rick.

The Doctor jumped up so quickly that his chair fell over.

'Show me,' he said.

Something strange was happening to the book underneath Rick's bed. It was beginning to quiver and twitch, like something coming back to life after a long, enforced sleep. The reddish-brown material which covered it rippled like slug-flesh jabbed with a stick. Tiny sparks of green light began first to dance across it, and then to coalesce, to form a jagged, spidery network of strands, rather like a flickering green web.

The web of light spread across the book, around it, and within moments had enshrouded it completely. It glowed brighter – so brightly, in fact, that soon the book no longer seemed like a book at all, but simply a block of dazzling green luminescence. It filled Rick's room, radiating out from under his bed, reflecting off the plastic models arranged on his shelves, bouncing back from the computer screen. Then it began to dwindle, to fade and, in less than a minute, had vanished completely. And where the book had been, among the dust balls and dead spiders and discarded comic books, was suddenly nothing but an empty space.

THREE

Midnight was the time that Earl Clayton hated the most. The bars were closed and everyone was tucked up at home, safe and snug, with their families around them.

Not him, though. He *had* no family. June had died four years ago, and now the only thing waiting for him in the big draughty house that had been their home was silence and a cold bed. People kept offering him advice to get his life back on track – buy a dog, get a part-time job, take a holiday, see a doctor. But none of them understood how he really felt. None of them understood that June had *been* his life. He and June hadn't needed anybody else, which he guessed was why they had never had kids. And after he had retired they had had such plans to see the world – Venice, Paris, Tokyo, New Delhi.

But then she had upped and died on him. Just like that. And, even with all his years of training and practice, he hadn't been able to do a damn thing about it. And so he had started to drink. To forget. He had known it was wrong, but he hadn't cared. And now drinking had become a habit, something he couldn't break away from. Something he relied on.

He was walking, or rather staggering, home. The streets of Blackwood Falls were deserted and there was a peculiar green mist enveloping the town. Street lamps were little more than hazy glows through the murk. Halloween pumpkins on porches and stoops were distant smudges of orange light.

Earl hadn't felt scared since June had died; had thought he was *beyond* feeling scared, in fact, since the worst thing that *could* have happened to him had already happened, four years earlier. But right now he *was* scared, and the funny thing was he didn't know why. For some reason there was a sense of deep apprehension churning in his gut. All right, so he kept thinking he could see shapes looming in the mist – ghostly faces, squat figures – but surely it wasn't *that* which was scaring him? Even in his drunken state he knew that was only his imagination, only his unfocused eyes trying to make sense of the swirling formlessness around him. No, there was something else. Something in the air. He wondered if the town was under attack from some unknown enemy, if the mist contained some substance that worked on the fear centres of the brain. Chemical warfare? It was possible.

He was passing the cemetery when he heard a noise.

He stopped and listened. The mist was like a blanket, not only blurring everything, but muffling sound too. He had to stand for several seconds, utterly motionless, before he heard it again.

A scrabbling sound. A pattering sound. As if something was burrowing down into the earth – or rising out of it.

Earl took hold of the cold thin bars of the cemetery gate and peered through them. He could see nothing. Nothing but swirling green mist and the pale, diffuse glow of an overhead lamp further along the path, between the graves.

Should he investigate? It might *be* someone. Someone he could talk to. Someone who might help him overcome his growing sense of dread.

The cemetery gate was actually two gates, which opened in the centre. Earl pushed the left-hand one, wincing as it creaked. He could still hear the sound of scrabbling ahead of him, but it was intermittent. It would stop for a while, then start up again, as if whatever was causing it kept needing to rest. He wondered if it was a dog, digging for a bone.

Plenty of bones round here, he thought, and put a hand over his mouth to stifle a giggle.

He started to walk, his shoes making tiny crackling sounds on the path between the graves. The mist was so thick he couldn't see the church, except as a vague block of fuzzy darkness somewhere in the distance. Tombstones rose on either side of him, looming from the mist like the dwarfish figures he had kept imagining he was seeing earlier. The scrabbling was somewhere to his left. He would have to step off the path and walk on the soft ground between the graves to locate it.

He hesitated for three seconds, then stepped off the path. Part of him wanted to go home, crawl into bed and pull the covers over his head, but a greater part felt the need to reach the heart of the mystery. The closer he got to the source of the sound, however, the greater became his sense of dread. It was like a steel fist around his lungs, cutting off his air, making him dizzy and sick.

He hunched down behind a tombstone and forced himself to take several deep breaths. When he felt able to carry on, he did so in a semi-crouch, slipping from tombstone to tombstone, suddenly eager not to be seen. The sound of scrabbling was louder now. It surely couldn't be more than a few steps away. Pressing himself up against a tombstone, he swallowed, counted to three, then raised his head slowly and peered over the top.

He could see nothing out of the ordinary. Just some old graves covered in weeds. One of the graves had a crooked sapling sticking up out of the centre of it. The sapling was creaking back and forth in the wind…

… and then Earl realised that there *was* no wind.

Without warning, the five spindly branches jutting from the thin trunk of the sapling bent in the centre, then opened out again. Earl felt all the blood draining from his face as he suddenly realised what he was *really* looking at.

It was an arm, black and twig-thin. And the 'branches' were fingers – each one as long as his forearm; each one bony and segmented, like the legs of a lobster; each one tipped by a hooked, razor-sharp talon.

As he watched, too terrified to move, the ground heaved and a figure rose slowly out of the ground. It was fully nine feet tall and impossibly thin, and seemed to be clothed in a rotting patchwork of black, tattered rags. Its hands – its long, *long* taloned hands – were awful enough, but more terrifying still was its head. It was huge and pale and fleshy, with deep-set eyes and a wide, wide mouth filled with jagged teeth.

Soil fell from the creature, pattering to the ground, as it pushed itself up from the earth. Once it had fully emerged, it looked slowly around, its great head creaking from left to right. It seemed almost to hover above the ground as though it weighed nothing at all. When it moved its hands, Earl could hear its fingers clicking together like bones.

As the massive head swung slowly towards his hiding place, Earl ducked down. He was panting and sweating and shaking. All at once he felt stone-cold sober. He forced himself to count to three again and then tentatively raised his head once more.

To his horror the creature was drifting like a wraith towards the tombstone behind which he was crouching. And what was more, it was looking straight at him!

Whimpering in terror, Earl rose to his feet and stumbled away. His body felt heavy and awkward, as though he was wading through sludge. He could hear his heartbeat pounding in his ears, could feel his breath tearing at his throat. He slithered and blundered between the graves, disorientated by the mist. He had an idea that if only he could make it to the cemetery gates he would be safe.

More by luck than judgement, he spotted the

thin dark thread of the path between a pair of
tombstones. He staggered towards it like a marathon
runner towards the finishing line. Now he could see
the black arch of the cemetery gates ahead, wreathed
in mist. With every thumping step, he expected to
feel long, bony fingers folding around his shoulder,
yanking him back. He glanced behind him and saw
the creature still gliding after him, the ends of its
tattered rags trailing behind it. He turned back to
face the gates – and another of the creatures loomed
out of the mist, blocking his path.

Earl clumped to a stop, too terrified even to scream.
He was close enough to the second creature to smell
it. It smelled foul and pungent, like decomposing
fruit. Slowly the creature lifted a finger to its lipless
mouth, as though urging him to be quiet. Then it
used the same finger to slash a curious X symbol in
the hazy air between Earl and itself.

Instantly Earl became aware that something
odd and terrible was happening to his face. He felt
a tugging, a tightening, almost as if his skin was
reshaping itself. His eyes bulging in terror, he clapped
a hand to his mouth. He dropped to his knees as the
mist closed in around him.

Chris was lying in a small, enclosed space. It was so
dark he couldn't even see his hand in front of his

eyes. There were hard surfaces on either side of him, and one just a few inches above his face.

It was a box of some kind, and it was hot and stuffy. If he didn't get out soon he'd suffocate. He pushed at the underside of the lid, but it wouldn't budge. He felt himself starting to panic. *Stay calm*, he thought, *stay calm*.

Then he heard a sound, right above his face, on the other side of the lid. A dull, heavy thump that broke into a scratchy patter of smaller items coming to rest. There followed a moment of silence, then it came again. And suddenly he realised where he was, what was happening.

He was in a coffin and he was being buried alive!

He began to scream and flail in the desperate hope that someone would hear him. And all at once the lid gave way under his fists. It didn't crack or splinter, but became soft, pliable, like dough. He sat up, smothered in the stifling thickness of it, and eventually it slid away from his face and he was able to breathe, to see. It was still dark, but there was a faint, greenish glow coming from somewhere in front of him. In the wan light he could just make out the familiar contours of his room, and realised the light was coming from the window.

It had been a dream, that's all. Just a dumb dream.

Chris fell back onto his bed, heart beating hard, sweat drying on his forehead. He didn't usually have nightmares. Bad dreams were kid's stuff. But he wasn't a kid any more. He'd moved on from all that, he'd matured. Of course, he wouldn't tell anyone about this, especially not Rick. Rick was still into trick-or-treating and dressing up with his loser buddies. Let *him* have the stupid nightmares. He deserved them.

Chris got out of bed to fetch himself a glass of water. His nocturnal freak-out must have been something to do with this weird green mist that had descended on the town. It was cool in a way, he guessed, but at the same time it seemed to be putting everyone on edge. His dad had been snappy at dinner, and his mom had kept glancing at the window as if she expected to see someone out there, peering in at them.

He glugged two glasses of water from the tap in the bathroom, then carried another back to his room. It was 12.30, and the house seemed encased in the kind of thick, muffled silence you usually got only with a heavy snowfall. Before getting back into bed, he stopped at his window and peered out. The mist was thicker than ever now. He could only just make out the vague shape of the black tree at the bottom of the garden.

Then he gave a little start. There was a glowing green light down by the tree. It seemed to be hovering in the air, like a giant firefly, or maybe a candle someone was holding. But a candle with a *green* flame? Could that be an effect of the mist?

He placed the glass of water on his bedside table and got back into bed. But he couldn't stop thinking about the green light. There was something freaky about it. In truth, he didn't think it was a firefly *or* a candle. So what then?

Only one way to find out, a little voice murmured in his head.

'Aw, gee,' he groaned, as if he didn't have a choice, and threw back his bedclothes. He pulled on jeans, sneakers and sweatshirt and went downstairs. He briefly considered waking his dad, but what would he say – 'I saw a light in the garden'? Yeah, big deal. If there was nothing there, and Rick got to hear of it, Chris would never live it down.

So OK, he'd check this out and then he'd go back to bed. There would be nothing there. It would just be one of those weird little mysteries, quickly forgotten. In the morning it would probably even seem unreal enough for Chris to convince himself he'd been sleepy, half-dreaming. He walked quietly through the dark house and let himself out the back door.

The mist latched onto him straight away and curled around him like something alive. It was chilly, clammy, and now that he was down at ground level, it seemed much thicker. *So* thick, in fact, that he couldn't even make out the tree from here.

Neither could he see a light. He considered going back inside, but knew he wouldn't settle until he'd at least trudged down to the tree to satisfy himself there was nothing there. He took a deep breath and set off. It was only thirty paces, maybe less, but in this mist he felt oddly reluctant to stray even that far from the house.

He was maybe halfway there when the tree came into view as a vague shape through the murk. For some reason, he slowed his pace. Though Chris had never told anyone, the tree had always freaked him out, and even these days he tried to look at it as little as possible. He began to tread more carefully, trying to be as quiet as he could, though he didn't know – or maybe he just didn't *want* to know – what he thought might hear him. He was less than ten paces away when he realised there was something strange and different about the tree.

No, not the tree itself, but the area where it stood. Next to the black tree was another tree that Chris felt sure had never been there before. It was tall and thin and there was what looked like a roundish clump of foliage at the top of it.

Then the new tree moved. Not much, but enough to make Chris realise that it wasn't a tree at all.

Impossible as it seemed, it was a person. Someone very tall and thin with… no, it must be the swirling mist playing tricks with his eyes. The figure's head couldn't really be *that* big and wide, could it? Because if it was, how did the spindly neck support it?

Chris stood motionless, watching the figure. He was pretty sure he hadn't been spotted, and suddenly being seen by this… this *thing* was the last thing he wanted in the whole world. He saw the figure reach up with its hands (its impossibly *long* hands) and make a series of weird gestures in the air. And then it did something that made his blood run cold. It started to speak.

It wasn't the words that chilled Chris, though – he didn't understand them; they sounded old, Latin or something – it was the voice. It was breathy and childlike and kind of echoey, and it sounded totally, totally mad. It made the hairs stand up on the back of Chris's neck, made the liquid drain from his mouth. The *thing* – he couldn't now think of it as anything even remotely human – raised its arms high in the air and said something that sounded like 'Zagaraldas'.

Instantly it began to sink into the ground. It

was as if a fissure had opened in the earth and was smoothly drawing the creature down. Chris watched as it disappeared, inch by inch, almost as if it was descending in an elevator. It took maybe a minute for the thing to disappear completely. Last to go were the taloned fingertips of its upraised hands.

Chris stood for another five seconds, looking at the spot where the creature had stood, then he turned and ran. He ran as if the thing had burst back out of the earth and was loping after him. He didn't stop running until he was back in his room and in his bed, shuddering under the bedclothes.

'About a million channels to choose from,' Martha said, remote control in hand, 'and not one decent thing to watch.'

The Doctor didn't reply. He was standing by the window of Martha's hotel room, peering out into the darkness. His hands were in his pockets and he was rocking backwards and forwards on his heels.

'Are you gonna stand there all night?' she asked, turning off the TV.

'Probably,' he said gloomily.

'Good. Well… enjoy yourself. I might as well try and get some sleep.'

She didn't, though. She continued to lie on top of the bedclothes, her head propped on her hand. She didn't even take off her shoes. Being with the Doctor had taught her that she should always be ready to run somewhere at a moment's notice.

'What you thinking about?' she asked finally.

'Talk in your sleep, do you?' he said.

'All the time,' she said. 'Never shut up, me.'

'I've noticed.'

'My mum's fault, that is. Never stop asking questions, Martha, she always said to me. Always have an enquiring mind. Remember, Martha, she'd say, every day's a school day.'

In the window reflection, Martha saw the trace of a smile flicker across the Doctor's face.

'She never said that,' he said.

'She did so.'

'Your mother? I can't imagine her saying that.'

'Yeah, well, that's 'cos you don't really know her. You should get to know her better.'

He hunched his shoulders, gave a little shudder. 'No thanks. Been there, done that, got the bruises to prove it.'

'What do you mean, "been there, done that"?' Martha scoffed. 'You've only met my mum that one time, and then it was hardly—'

'It wasn't your mother I was talking about,' he said softly.

Martha went quiet. Ever since accompanying

the boys back to Rick's – thankfully managing to avoid bumping into his parents and all the awkward explanations that that would have involved – only to find that the mysterious book had disappeared, they'd been at a bit of a loose end. And whenever that happened, whenever they weren't dashing from one place to another, the conversation invariably seemed to turn towards the Doctor's ex-companion.

In an attempt to steer him away from that particular subject, she said, 'So what's our next move?'

He made an exasperated sound with his lips. She knew how much he hated mooching around, biding his time. He always had to *be* somewhere, *doing* something. She, however, was a mere mortal and, however much she loved being with him, she was glad of the occasional rest, the chance to recharge her batteries.

'Back to Rick's first thing in the morning, speak to his brother, see if he's got this book,' he said. He rocked forward until his head hit the window with a thump that made Martha wince. 'It's a jigsaw piece,' he muttered.

'The book?'

He nodded. It looked as though he was cleaning the window with his fringe. 'It's a stonking great jigsaw piece. It's probably the piece that sits right in the middle, and I bet it's got an eye or a hat on it or something.'

'OK,' she said, thinking about the analogy, 'but even if we had that piece we still wouldn't have the box with the picture on it, would we?'

'Nah, but we could probably work the picture out from the other pieces – the energy splurge, the tree, the defence thingies, this mist…' He rocked himself back again and started pacing up and down like a caged animal. 'Even with the pieces we've got, it should mean *something*.' He whapped his forehead three times with the flat of his hand. 'Come on, think, think, think.'

He stopped again by the window, looked out, and suddenly became very still.

'What is it?' asked Martha.

'Look at this,' he said quietly.

She jumped to her feet and joined him at the window. In the greenish murk below was an old man. He was staggering around in circles, one hand clamped over the lower half of his face, the other waving blindly about in front of him.

'Someone's had one too many,' Martha said.

'I don't think he's drunk,' murmured the Doctor.

As they watched, the old man spun in a final clumsy pirouette and crumpled to the ground. Suddenly the Doctor was running for the door.

'Come on.'

He thundered down the stairs, Martha in hot pursuit. Despite its name, the Falls Palace was only a small hotel, family-run, less than a dozen rooms. The owner, Eloise Walsh, a grey-haired, no-nonsense woman who wore half-moon spectacles, attached to a chain, perched on the end of her nose, was manning the front desk, and looked up in indignation as the Doctor swept past.

'Hey, what's the—'

'Man down!' yelled the Doctor, yanking open the main door without even breaking stride.

The old man was sitting in the street, hunched forward, rocking back and forth like a distressed toddler.

Martha saw immediately that the Doctor had been right. The man wasn't merely drunk. It was evident from his panicky eyes that he was scared out of his wits. He still had a hand clamped over the lower half of his face, as if whatever he had seen was too terrible to speak of.

The Doctor dropped to one knee beside him. 'Hey there, feller,' he said softly, reaching out. The old man flinched back and the Doctor murmured, 'It's all right, I'm not going to hurt you.'

'That's Earl Clayton,' said a voice from behind Martha. She looked round to see Eloise Walsh standing at her shoulder. 'What's wrong with him – aside from the usual?'

The Doctor ignored her. He was speaking directly into Clayton's ear, his voice so low that Martha couldn't make out what he was saying. His words didn't appear to have any effect, however, until he touched the centre of Clayton's forehead with the tip of his right index finger.

Instantly the old man relaxed, the tension leaving his shoulders, his hand dropping away from his face.

When she saw what had been done to him, Martha gasped.

'Merciful Father!' blurted Eloise Walsh and swiftly crossed herself.

The Doctor looked grimly appalled. He placed a hand on the old man's shoulder and murmured, 'I'm so sorry. We'll find who did this, I promise.'

Clayton gazed up at them and made no attempt to speak. Martha wondered whether that was simply because he couldn't, or because he had actually realised that he no longer had a mouth.

FOUR

I am not scared, Martha told herself, *I am not scared, I am not scared.*

'You're scared, aren't you?' said the Doctor.

'No!' she said, too loudly and too quickly.

'Yes you are. And shall I tell you *why* you are?'

'Is it because fear is a sign of intelligence?' she said hopefully.

He wrinkled his nose in apology. 'Oh, I wish I could say yes. But no, that's not it. The reason you're scared is because I was wrong.'

'Wrong?' she said. 'You?'

He held up his hands. 'Yeah, yeah, I know, hard to believe, genius and all that. Though when I say *wrong*, perhaps I'm being a bit melodramatic. It might be more accurate to say I can see more of the big picture now.'

'Are we talking about jigsaws again?' she asked.

'Mm, kind of, I s'pose. Remember when you asked if the mist was toxic, and I said it wasn't?'

Martha didn't like where this was leading. They were currently walking *through* the mist; they were surrounded by it, *wreathed* in it. 'Ye-es,' she said guardedly.

'Well, that's the bit I was wrong about.'

'You mean to say it *is* toxic?' She put out a hand and grabbed the sleeve of his long coat. 'Oh, suddenly I don't feel so well. I'm sure there's a burning sensation at the back of my throat. That's indicative of—'

'Oh, yeah,' the Doctor butted in cheerfully, swirling a hand in the green mist. 'Poison, this stuff is. Only it doesn't affect your body.'

'Doesn't it?'

'No.' He tapped the side of his temple with a long forefinger. 'It affects your mind. Works its nasty way down all those primitive little channels to all those dank little rooms where we keep our phobias and fears. And then it throws open the doors and lets 'em all out. There's the storming of the Bastille going on in that noggin of yours, Martha Jones. Though to be fair,' he conceded wistfully, 'the storming of the Bastille wasn't as impressive as the French would have us believe. It wasn't actually much of a *storming*, more a kind of… light drizzle.'

'I think I feel a bit better now,' said Martha.

He gave an exaggerated wink. 'That's my girl!'

'Still quite scared, though,' she said.

'Yeah, well, that's OK,' he replied. 'Fear is a sign of intelligence.'

They were retracing Earl Clayton's steps in an attempt to discover what had happened to him. Despite her brusqueness, Eloise Walsh had taken the old man under her scrawny wing. She had told the Doctor and Martha that Earl lived in the big house at the end of Harrows Lane and that he always followed the same route home after a night's drinking. The Doctor and Martha had been following her directions for over ten minutes, but so far all was quiet. In fact, they hadn't come across a single soul since leaving the hotel. Martha thought that the good people of Blackwood Falls obviously had more sense than to venture out in a pea-souper like this.

'Have you come across many mouth-removing aliens before?' she asked, hoping a chat would allay her nervousness.

'Not many, no,' said the Doctor. 'Came across one not long ago that took whole faces.'

'Maybe this is that one's little brother or something,' she suggested.

'Nah, the methodology's completely different.'

'Will Mr Clayton recover, do you think?'

'He will if I have anything to do with it,' said the Doctor grimly.

'What if that thing does to us what it did to him?' she asked.

'Ha! I'd like to see it try and shut *me* up.'

They were passing a pair of tall, black, wrought-iron gates. In the murk beyond, Martha could see a thread of path weaving between flanking expanses of grass, from which loomed the vague suggestions of gravestones.

The Doctor stopped. 'I see a light.'

'Actually or metaphorically?' asked Martha.

He pointed through the bars of the gate. 'In there.'

'I can't see anything,' she said.

'It's gone now. But it was there. Come on, let's have a look.'

The gate creaked as they pulled it open.

'Well,' said Martha, '*that* was inevitable.'

The Doctor grinned at her and strolled casually ahead, sonic at the ready. The green mist swirled around them. Martha kept seeing shapes in it, which she informed herself firmly were all in her mind. Soon the black gates were no longer visible, and she couldn't help thinking that it was as though they'd been denied their only escape route. Suddenly, in the gloom to her right, she saw a yellowish blur.

'Was that—' she began, but the Doctor was already striding off through the grass between the gravestones. 'Obviously it was,' she muttered.

The mist was like an endless series of green curtains, parting to allow them access, then closing again behind them. As they neared the place where the yellowish blur had come from, they saw it a second time, and then a third, an eerie and mysterious wraith-like glow, which gradually resolved itself into something thankfully more mundane – a cone of mist-diffused light cast by a bobbing torch.

Seconds later they saw the vague outline of the person holding the torch. It was an old lady with straggly white hair, a long black skirt and a grey shawl like a dense swathe of cobwebs. There was a black cat prowling at her heels, and Martha's heart skipped a beat. Not witches again, she thought. She'd had enough witches to last her a lifetime.

The old lady had her back to them and was leaning over, looking down at something. The Doctor walked right up beside her and leaned over too.

'That's interesting,' he said conversationally.

He was peering into what looked to Martha like a rabbit burrow, quite narrow but so deep that she couldn't see the bottom, even though the old lady was shining her torch into it. The old lady turned to look at the Doctor, and Martha was relieved to see that her profile was not witchy at all. She was plump and bespectacled, with a perfectly normal nose and chin.

'Who are you?' she asked, as if the Doctor was intruding on her property.

'Is that *really* the most pertinent question you should be asking right now?' he said blandly.

She looked taken aback, but recovered quickly. Eyes flashing, she said, 'What are you doing here?'

'*That's* the one!' he said, and for a moment Martha thought he was going to slap the old lady on the back. Then his voice became sombre. 'We're investigating.'

'Investigating what?'

'We're trying to find out who attacked Earl Clayton,' said Martha.

The old lady looked over her shoulder and fixed Martha with a fierce stare. 'Earl's been attacked? How is he?'

'He'll live,' muttered the Doctor.

'So what are *you* doing here?' Martha asked, and tried not to look too pleased at the Doctor's expression of approval.

The old lady's eyes narrowed. She glanced at the Doctor. 'Who's she? Your floozy?'

The Doctor looked at Martha, his face adopting an expression of wide-eyed innocence. In an equally innocent voice he asked, 'Are you my floozy, Martha?'

'I'm nobody's floozy,' Martha said, bridling.

'She says she's nobody's floozy,' the Doctor said.

The old lady hmphed as if she didn't believe a word of it.

'And she did ask a very good question,' the Doctor continued. 'What *are* you doing here?'

The old lady seemed to puff herself up. Almost defiantly she said, 'I was drawn here. I felt that something was wrong.'

The Doctor's expression hadn't changed, but Martha could almost hear the cogs whirring in his head. 'Really?' he said. 'Now that's even *more* interesting.'

Although Martha hadn't seen him do it, the Doctor had put his sonic screwdriver away when they had encountered the old lady. Now he whipped it out again and examined the hole with it.

The old lady watched him for a moment and then asked, 'What's that?'

'It's an alien device,' said the Doctor casually, though Martha could see that he was watching her reaction out of the corner of his eye.

She was silent for a moment, then she sniffed. 'You from outer space then?'

He shrugged. 'Could be.'

She turned to Martha. 'Are *you* from outer space too?'

'No,' said Martha, 'I'm from London.'

All at once the sonic began to emit a high-pitched, warbling shriek. The black cat yowled and ran away.

'Uh-oh,' said the Doctor quietly.

'What?' said Martha.

'They know we're here.'

'Who do?' asked the old lady.

'Whoever dug this hole.'

He turned the sonic off, jumped to his feet and spun around. This time Martha's eyes were not playing tricks on her. Something odd was happening.

Several mini-whirlwinds had sprung up among the mist-shrouded tombstones. They were ranging about like spinning tops, gathering up autumn leaves which were strewn about on the ground. Within seconds the whirlwinds had not only collected every leaf in the immediate vicinity, but had started to *mould* them into half a dozen roughly humanoid shapes, with thick stubby limbs and vaguely spherical heads.

Martha watched in horrified fascination as, with an eerie crackling of dry leaves, the closest of the whirlwind-figures raised one of its lumpen hands and pointed at her.

Next moment she was aware of something spinning towards her face. She ducked instinctively and the spinning object – *a leaf*, she realised in amazement – whipped past, though not before the tip of it had grazed her cheekbone and opened a thin, stinging cut.

'Cover your heads!' shouted the Doctor, turning up the collar of his coat as the leaf-creatures ambled towards them with a dry scraping sound. Martha pulled her jacket up over her black hair as all six of the creatures raised their arms and unleashed a flurry of razor-sharp leaves. She was half-aware of the old lady beside the Doctor flipping her grey shawl over her head, and then all three of them were running across the grass, taking care not to collide with the tombstones, which seemed to be rising out of the green mist in front of them, like obstacles conjured by their pursuers.

Martha felt several leaves slice across the skin of her hands as she ran, leaving stripes of blood in their wake. Fleeing for the gates, leaves slashing and swooping around them, she was half-aware of the Doctor frantically searching his pockets.

Suddenly he shouted, 'Aha!' and held aloft a packet of crisps.

'All this exercise making you a bit peckish, is it?' she yelled.

His long legs still carrying him unerringly through the obstacle course of gravestones, the Doctor tore open the bag and started rooting through it, tossing crisps left and right with wild abandon. Finally he found what he was looking for: a little blue sachet of salt. Stuffing the empty bag back into his pocket, he tore open the sachet with his teeth and emptied the salt into his cupped hand. He muttered something, then flung the salt over his shoulder.

Instantly the storm of murderous leaves swirling around them fluttered harmlessly to the ground. Martha glanced back just in time to see the leaf-creatures collapse into half a dozen lifeless mounds. The Doctor had turned and was running back towards the nearest of the mounds. As Martha thumped to a halt, panting, he thrust his sonic into it.

'Nothing,' he said, 'just leaves.' He scattered them with a kick.

Martha bent at the waist, hands on knees, gasping with adrenalin. She was impressed to see that not only had the old lady managed to keep up with them, but she was barely out of breath.

'What did you do?' Martha asked the Doctor.

'I chucked some salt at them,' he said.

'Yeah, I could see that, but... why?'

The Doctor looked at the old lady and raised his eyebrows as if inviting her to answer.

'Natural occult defence,' she said, as if it was obvious.

'Very good,' he said, giving her one of his goofy grins. 'You know your stuff. What did you say your name was again?'

'I didn't,' she said waspishly, and then abruptly her expression softened. 'But it's Etta. Etta Helligan.'

'Pleased to meet you, Etta Helligan,' said the Doctor, shaking her hand. 'I'm the Doctor and this is Martha.'

'You said occult,' pointed out Martha. 'Like magic, you mean?'

'Or a science so ancient and arcane it *seems* like magic,' he said.

Martha remembered her initial thought when she had seen the old woman. 'Is it the Carrionites again?'

The Doctor shook his head. 'No, this isn't their style. Too elaborate. Too theatrical.'

'And you're saying Shakespeare *wasn't* theatrical?' Martha said.

Another grin. 'Good point, well made.'

Etta Helligan watched this exchange with interest. 'Why are you people here?' she asked.

The Doctor tossed his sonic into the air, caught it and slipped it into his pocket. 'We're here to help,' he said.

'Intergalactic emergency services, that's us,' commented Martha drily.

The Doctor suddenly leaned forward, peering intently into Etta's face. 'You're old, aren't you?' he said. He turned, wincing indignantly, as Martha punched him sharply in the back. Then his face cleared. 'Was that rude?' He swung back to Etta. 'I'm sorry, that was rude, wasn't it? What I meant was… um… you've probably lived here a long time? You know a lot about the town? About its history?'

'My great-great-great grandparents were one of the founding families,' she told him proudly.

'Well… great!' he said. 'Let's go back to yours then, for a chat. And preferably some cocoa.'

'You're a very forward young man, aren't you?' she said.

'Forward, backward, sideways. Half the time I don't know whether I'm coming or going.'

Etta raised an eyebrow and turned to Martha. 'Is he always like this?'

'No,' said Martha. 'Sometimes he can be quite eccentric.'

Etta laughed, and suddenly Martha could see the young woman she had once been. 'Is that so? Then your life must be very interesting, Martha.'

'Oh, yeah,' said Martha, smiling back at her, 'it's certainly that.'

FIVE

The chamber was deep underground, and filled with a ceaseless, insectile rustling. Bulbous growths tumesced from the undulating walls; nodular columns and contorted pedestals, black and jagged and somehow sinewy, jutted from the uneven floor.

To an untrained eye, these strange, twisted shapes might have resembled the remains of lightning-blasted trees, or could even have been mistaken as the manifestation of some mad sculptor's fevered imaginings.

What they actually were, however, were the products of alien technology. And although they *appeared* inert, each separate component, and indeed the very fabric of the chamber, was threaded with a network of what appeared to be veins, through which pulsed – like sluggish, poisonous blood – a faint, green light.

Dominating the centre of the chamber was a dais that was almost the height of a man, from which sprouted a dozen or more vine-like tendrils, connected to the walls on either side. A hollow appeared to have been scooped from the tangled knot of worm-like roots in the flattened crown of the dais, and in this hollow nestled the book that Rick and his friends had dug out from under the black tree.

Silently a stream of figures drifted into the chamber and formed a wide circle around the dais. The figures were impossibly tall and spindly, with long, taloned fingers and massive, squashy, hairless heads. Even in this dank, windless place, their black rags seemed to float around their elongated bodies like the fronds of undersea plants. The last of the figures to enter the chamber appeared to be their leader, even though its appearance seemed all but identical to the others. It was this figure, however, which stood before the book and placed the hooked tips of its many-jointed fingers on the fleshy cover. It was this figure too which began to speak, or rather chant, words that seemed ancient and alien and somehow ominous. The creature's voice, echoing around the chamber, was breathy, sing-song, almost giggly. It was the voice of a child that was sweetly and dangerously mad.

As it had in Rick's room, the book began to writhe and quiver, like something alive. Sparks of green light flickered and danced about its surface, and as each spark formed it was sucked greedily away by the chamber itself. However, this didn't diminish the power of the book. On the contrary, as the chanting continued, the light produced by it gradually strengthened in both brightness and volume. Soon green light was flowing from the book like mother's milk flowing into the bellies of many children. It flowed down the dais and radiated out across the floor in great gulping surges; it flowed through the tendrils attached to the dais and into the walls; it flowed into the nodular growths and contorted pedestals, invigorating them. The spindly figures looked around, grinning their horribly wide, jagged-toothed grins. They hissed in ecstasy and clicked their long, segmented fingers as the chamber came to glowing life around them.

When the chamber had drunk its fill, the leader of the figures raised its right arm and turned its hand palm upwards, the fingers unfurling slowly like the legs of a massive, awakening spider. As if responding to this movement, a bubble of swirling light formed in the centre of the book and then rose slowly into the air before nestling into the palm of the leader's outstretched hand. The leader brought the hand close to its massive mouth, as if to swallow the ball of light. Instead, however, the creature whispered a further incantation, almost as though giving the light instructions. Finally the leader stretched out an arm, raising its hand high above its bulbous head. The ball of light sat there for a moment, and then, as if propelled by some arcane purpose, it drifted away...

Jim Tozier had decided this was to be his last Halloween. He'd struggled on for three years with Tozier's Costume Emporium since Glenn had died, but his heart just wasn't in it any more. It was Jim's dad, Pete, who had started the business in the 1950s, and Jim himself had taken over the reins in 1978, when the old man retired. Jim had met Glenn whilst on holiday in Florida in 1983 and, though Glenn had become a partner in the business – with Dad's blessing – a year later, and had worked side-by-side with Jim for the next twenty happy years, it was Glenn himself who had insisted that Jim keep the store's original name.

'TCE is an institution in the Falls,' he would say.

'Yeah, but so's the sanatorium up on Blackwood Hill,' Jim would joke.

Secretly, though, Jim had been glad not to have to change the name. It wasn't that he didn't want to acknowledge Glenn's contribution (he loved the man, and would sing his praises whenever he could), it was simply that Tozier & Reid's Costume Emporium sounded kind of long-winded. Besides, it wouldn't have stopped folk still calling the place Tozier's out of habit, and neither would it have made folk any more nor less aware of what he and Glenn meant to each other. And so the name had stayed, and Glenn had stayed, and – apart from his dad's death in '99 – the next two decades had been the happiest of Jim's life.

But then in 2004 all those years of smoking (thirty a day from the age of fifteen) had finally caught up with Glenn and, on 15 December 2005, with Glenn insisting he would hang on for one more Christmas, the Good Lord had taken him for a sunbeam. People couldn't have been kinder to Jim, and maybe for the first time he had discovered what good and loyal friends he had in the Falls, but even so the weeks and months and now years following Glenn's death had been nothing but a struggle.

So now here he was, not too far from the big six-oh, and every day the voice urging him to pack his bags and head out to Vancouver grew louder and louder. His sister, Mary, and her family were out there, and for the past couple of years they had been trying to get him to sell up and join them in what, Mary was constantly telling him, was the world's third most liveable city.

It was only last week that he had finally come to the decision he had been leaning towards for the past six months, only last week that he had decided the For Sale signs would be going up the Monday after Halloween. It was kind of sad in a way, but exciting too. Jim had already called Mary and asked her to start looking for an apartment he could buy, had already started planning his new life.

Maybe it was this – the anticipation, the apprehension – that was making it so tough to sleep tonight. Or maybe it was this damn weird mist that seemed to be making the atmosphere heavy, oppressive.

He looked out of his bedroom window, having woken from his fitful sleep for maybe the fifth time in the past two hours. He had certainly never seen mist this colour before. It was eerie, like something out of a horror movie. Jim hoped there wasn't something sinister about it, hoped the mist wasn't the result of some poisonous gas leak or something. He was a sensible man, and was not generally given to such wild speculation, but there was just something... well, *not right* about this.

In the dressing-table mirror across the room, he caught a glimpse of himself sitting on the edge of the bed, and the sudden unexpectedness of seeing his reflection shocked him. Heck, when had he gotten so *fat*? He'd always been a big guy, but he hadn't realised his belly had become *quite* so huge. With his thick white moustache and round-lensed spectacles, all he'd have to do was grow a bushy white beard and he'd be the spit of Santa Claus.

He was resting his hands ruefully on the stretched T-shirt over his belly and wondering about maybe shedding a few pounds before embarking on his new life when he heard a noise downstairs. It was a vague noise, hard to pinpoint. Kind of a bump, kind of a scuff. The sound of something falling over maybe... or of some*one* moving around.

Jim's heart began to thump harder. Maybe it was this that was making him so restless tonight – the feeling that he was not alone. It was weird, but now that his mind had latched onto that thought, it didn't want to let it go. He had a sudden, almost overwhelming conviction that someone was downstairs, moving around among the costumes. Someone who was up to no good. His imagination started to go into overdrive. He pictured a cowled figure brandishing a big, shiny knife.

Stop it, he told himself firmly, *you're being ridiculous.*

Even so, he pulled on jeans, shoes and a sweater before heading downstairs. If there *was* someone down there, he would feel a little vulnerable dressed only in boxers and a T-shirt. He wondered about taking something to defend himself with, but couldn't think of anything appropriate. He didn't own a gun and he would never dream of using a knife. Plus he was neither a golfer nor a baseball player. In the end he settled on the long, heavy flashlight with the rubber grip he kept with his tools in the cupboard under the kitchen sink. If the worst came to the worst, he could rap any potential assailant over the head with it.

Not that he would need to, he told himself.

The building was over a hundred years old, and the stairs leading down from his apartment to the shop creaked. Jim winced the first time it happened, but by the third or fourth he had come to terms with the fact that he had well and truly lost the element of surprise. He clomped down the remaining steps and slid free the bolts on the door at the bottom. Bracing himself, he shoved the door open and shone his flashlight directly in front of him at face height. That way, if some ravening lunatic came at him he might dazzle them long enough to overpower them, or at least get away.

But no one came at him. The shop was quiet and

empty. *Seemed* quiet and empty. Shining his flashlight around, he couldn't deny there were plenty of places where a potential burglar

(*or psycho*)

might hide.

Take that rack of costumes over by the right-hand wall, for instance. Was it his imagination, or had he seen them move just a little, as if stirred by a non-existent breeze? And the Halloween masks displayed on pegs above the counter. They'd never bothered him before, but now he couldn't shake off the feeling that they were watching him. And then there was the Evil Clown costume in the front window, draped over Sam the Mannequin. It was facing front, designed to leer at potential customers who might be passing by the store, but when Jim's flashlight beam swept across it, didn't he see it move its head just a little? Didn't he see the faintest flicker from its floppy orange hair? Didn't he see an odd greenish glint in the empty eye socket of its grinning rubber face?

He shuddered and realised his mouth was very dry. Too dry to issue a challenge to whoever

(*or whatever*)

might be lurking in the shadows.

Aware that he was behaving like a frightened child, aware that he hadn't let his imagination run this wild since he was about twelve, Jim stomped across the room to the light switch by the door. As he did so he saw, out of the corner of his eye, the Evil Clown turn its head to follow his progress. Heart leaping, he swung his flashlight towards it. No, he had been mistaken. The clown was still facing front. It hadn't moved at all.

He reached the light switch and jabbed it with a sweaty finger. Darkness was instantly dispelled. Shadow-clotted hiding places became harmless nooks and crannies. Jim breathed a little easier. As though attracted by the light, the green mist outside seemed to curl and drift towards the door, to press itself against the glass panels. Jim told himself he couldn't see shapes in it. Told himself he couldn't see a pair of blurry hands squashing themselves against the glass, or a fat, doughy face with a yawning mouth peering in at him.

Averting his eyes from the swirling greenness outside, he quickly searched the shop. There was nobody here. No one lurking between the costumes, no one hiding behind the counter. The masks were just masks and the Evil Clown in the window was just rubber and material draped over a tatty old mannequin that had been here since his father's day.

Though he was alone, Jim felt a bit embarrassed.

He could imagine how Glenn would have hooted at his nervousness.

'Yeah, yeah, I know,' Jim muttered, glancing towards the ceiling as if Glenn was up there somewhere, watching over him.

He turned off the lights and clumped back up to bed. Yessir, he thought to himself, this was definitely going to be his last Halloween.

Jim Tozier was not the only person in Blackwood Falls who was finding sleep hard to come by that night. Across town, 12-year-old Rick Pirelli was tossing and turning fitfully in bed, his sheets a sweaty tangle around his feet. His eyelids flickered and he muttered to himself. He kept drifting in and out of wakefulness, though for the most part seemed to be hovering in a kind of limbo, where dreams and reality were knotted together so tightly it seemed impossible to pick them apart. In his mind's eye he kept seeing the book, kept feeling its binding squirm under his fingers like flesh. Then he was standing by the black tree. Then he was digging beneath it, sliding down between its roots into a stinking, filthy tunnel. Then he was fighting his way through green mist, trying to find his way home. But the mist was getting into his lungs and choking him, stinging his eyes and clamping itself to his face like clammy hands. He fought against it, but it wound itself around his legs like rope. And then Rick was back in his room, in his bed, and it should have been dark, but it wasn't, because the room was lit by a sickly green glow. The glow was coming from the eyes of the werewolf costume he had collected from Tozier's that day, and which was now hanging on the back of his door like the pelt of some savage animal. As Rick stared at the costume, it slowly turned its sagging, frozen snarl of a face towards him. He cowered in terror beneath the pitiless scrutiny of its blazing virescent eyes…

… and woke, gasping, sweat or possibly tears running down his cheeks.

It was dark in his room. There was no green glow. Rick looked across at the black, lumpy shape of the costume hanging on his door. It wasn't moving. Of *course* it wasn't. It was lifeless as an old coat. He stretched out a trembling hand and turned on his nitelight. It was a revolving one, Superman flying above the spires of Metropolis. A bit childish, he guessed, but Rick liked it. It made him feel secure somehow, made him feel that with Superman by his side he was safe from the monsters.

That weird guy, the Doctor, had given him a similar feeling. Not that he was a superhero or anything. He just seemed like the sort of guy you'd turn to if…

If what?

If the monsters really did show up, a little voice whispered in his head before he could stop it.

Rick settled back down into his bed and pulled the covers up to his chin. With Superman patrolling the skies beside him, he closed his eyes.

But it was a long time before he slept.

'So tell me about the tree,' said the Doctor.

He was sitting in a squashy old armchair, one hand wrapped around a mug of hot chocolate, the other scratching the head of a ginger tom cat curled in his lap. He'd once said something about not being keen on cats, but he seemed to be getting on OK with this one. Not that he had much choice. They were everywhere in Etta's rambling old house, purring and prowling and slinking around their heels. Martha was just glad that she wasn't allergic.

Etta, sitting on a sofa adjacent to a crackling log fire that was filling the high-ceilinged, book-lined room with the sweet scent of wood smoke, spread her chubby, wrinkled hands. 'What's to tell? It's old. Older than old. According to the Niantic, it's been here for centuries.'

'Niantic?' queried Martha.

'The indigenous peoples of this area.'

'And your ancestors named the town after it?' the Doctor said.

Etta nodded. 'They used it as a kind of... focal point, I guess. Built the town around it.'

'But why Falls?' the Doctor asked. 'I mean, the Blackwood bit's obvious, but why Falls? Is there a waterfall around here?'

'It's not that,' said Etta. 'The Niantics believed that the tree didn't grow from the ground but fell from the sky. They believe it hit the ground with such force that it buried itself deep in the earth. So deep that the roots pierced the spirit-world and released a tribe of cannibal spirits called Hee-oko.'

'Hee-oko,' the Doctor murmured, a fiercely intense expression on his face.

'What is it, Doctor?' Martha asked. 'More jigsaw pieces?'

He was staring into the middle distance, evidently thinking hard. 'Mmm,' he said, 'and I don't think I like the picture I'm starting to see.' Abruptly his head jerked up, as if he was waking from a trance, and he stared at Etta. 'I'm guessing the roots of that tree extend right under your property, yes?'

She shrugged. 'I suppose. But what of it?'

'I'm also guessing,' he continued, 'that the members of your family who've lived in this house have had—' he waggled the fingers of both hands at the sides of his head '—lots of weirdy brain stuff going on? Second sight, that kind of thing?'

Now Etta looked a bit more impressed. 'It's true that we've been blessed with certain psychic gifts,' she conceded.

'Knew it!' he shouted, jumping up and spilling the startled tom cat onto the floor. It gave a yowl of protest and stalked out of the room, tail in the air. The Doctor raised his head and sniffed as if he could smell something burning. 'That pong is unmistakeable. And my teeth are itching again. Can you smell it, Martha?'

'I can smell cat pee, if that's what you mean,' she muttered under her breath.

'Residual psychic energy!' he exclaimed. 'It's all over the place. This house is *steeped* in it.'

'Is it dangerous?' asked Etta, glancing around nervously as if she expected to be able to see what he was talking about, like patches of dry rot staining the walls.

'Won't do you any harm,' said the Doctor. 'If anything, it's good for you. Invigorates the old grey matter. Bet you've never had any village idiots in your clan.'

'I should say not,' said Etta a little stuffily.

The Doctor held up his sonic screwdriver. 'Mind if I do a bit of sonicking? Just to see what's what?'

Etta waved an imperious hand. 'Be my guest.'

The Doctor grinned and turned the sonic on. The

tip glowed a brilliant, dazzling blue.

In the black chamber, the softly pulsing green light that trickled through the veins of the place like life-blood suddenly became more agitated. The spindly giants drifting about the room, tending to various items of equipment, stopped what they were doing. One by one, their great heads creaked round and the glinting caverns of their deep-set eyes focused on the central dais. The book was convulsing in its fibrous mounting like a fibrillating heart, jagged threads of green light skittering across its surface. The leader of the creatures hissed and moved forward, placing its hands on the book. It uttered a series of alien words and phrases in its sing-song voice. The light gathered itself into a crackling knot, then leaped from the book into its hands. The leader opened its vast mouth wide, exposing rows of viciously pointed teeth, and let loose a breathy ululation of sound that might have been a war cry. It opened its hands and released the spitting orb of light. The light rose into the air, shedding sparks, and then with a sudden, furious flash it disappeared.

Followed by Martha and a somewhat bewildered Etta, the Doctor wandered around the ground floor of the old lady's house, sonic held out before him.

Occasionally he would stop to thrust the device at, or into, something – a portrait of a sombre-looking man with mutton-chop whiskers in the hallway; an Ormulu clock; a basket of slightly wrinkly fruit on the dining table. Several times he stopped and doubled back, pushing between Martha and Etta as if they weren't there, eliciting *tsks* of annoyance from the old woman. Once, he dropped to his knees so abruptly that Martha winced, and pressed his ear to the scuffed floorboards like a Native American tracker in an old cowboy movie.

'Have you found something?' Martha asked after she and Etta had stood there patiently for thirty seconds while he tapped and hmmed and listened.

'There's a boll weevil down there,' he said, jumping up. 'It's a long way from home and it's got a nasty cough. Poor little feller.'

Martha and Etta exchanged a look. It was clear the old lady was growing impatient.

'Yes, but have you found anything… relevant?' Martha said.

'Relevance is relative,' replied the Doctor, 'and try saying that three times quickly after a bottle of sambuca.' He strode off again, sonicking all over the place. 'Thing is, it's a hard one to pinpoint. The fabric of the house has been soaking this stuff up for so many years that the entry point is hidden. It's like looking for a red ball in a sea of identical red balls. Impossible.'

'So what's the point?' snapped Etta. 'Sounds to me like you might as well quit.'

'*Quit?*' exclaimed the Doctor, horrified. 'Just because something's impossible that's no reason to quit. I happen to *like* impossible. Impossible's a challenge. Any old chancer can do *almost* impossible, but the real thing, the genuine article... that's the one that sorts the legends from the wannabes. Oh.'

He had been striding about as he was talking, but now, at the bottom of the wide staircase, he stopped dead and looked up. A black cat was crouched on the top step, fur standing up on its body, glaring balefully down at them.

'I don't like the look of *that*,' he said quietly.

'Oh, that's just Romeo,' said Etta.

'I think the Doctor's referring to the way the cat's eyes are glowing green,' said Martha. 'My guess is they're not supposed to do that.'

Romeo hissed at them. Out of the corner of her eye, Martha sensed movement, and turned to see another cat slinking along the hallway. This one was long-haired, its rust-coloured coat streaked with black, and its eyes too were glowing with an unnatural green light.

Next moment the ginger tom that had been sitting

on the Doctor's lap darted out from the doorway of the dining room across the entrance hall, and was immediately followed by a dainty white female. The light that filled both cats' eyes was swirling sluggishly, like a luminous version of the mist outside. It was a thick, soupy, somehow *putrescent* light. Martha wasn't sure why, but for some reason it made her think of things that were dead and rotting.

'They're possessed, aren't they?' she whispered to the Doctor.

'Well, I prefer to think of it as holistic subjugation, which doesn't necessarily denote—'

'*Doctor!*' Martha screamed.

The black cat had launched itself at them from the top step, a yowling black missile of teeth and claws. In a flash, the Doctor grabbed Martha and Etta and swung them behind him, snapping back his head as Romeo sailed past his face, taking a swipe at him and missing his nose by inches. The cat landed on its feet and immediately turned to confront them again. And now more cats were appearing from above and around them, a bristling, screeching legion of vicious teeth, unsheathed claws and blazing green eyes.

'Run!' the Doctor yelled, and bustled the two women ahead of him along the corridor that ran parallel with the staircase. But they had taken no more than a few steps when the kitchen door at the end of the corridor was nudged open and a further wave of cats came streaming out, eyes burning with green fire.

Now there were cats both at their heels and ahead of them. Using his body as a shield, the Doctor pulled Martha and Etta behind him again. All three of them backed towards the wall of wood panelling that ran up the side of the staircase. Once again the Doctor produced his sonic screwdriver and held it up like a weapon, swinging it from left to right. Behind him, Martha and Etta pressed themselves into his back. Martha raised her hands to protect her face as the cats closed in…

SIX

Something was jabbing Martha in the back, but she was so focused on the advancing army of cats that at first she didn't register its significance. Then it struck her: she was leaning against a doorknob. She twisted round in the confined space between the Doctor and the wall and realised there was a door literally carved into the wood panelling. The reason she hadn't noticed it before – aside from the fact she'd been preoccupied with not getting her face scratched off by a mob of possessed felines – was because the door was so flush with its frame that it was easy to overlook. Even the doorknob wasn't much bigger than a walnut. She curled her hand around it and gave it a tug and the door popped open.

'In here,' she hissed. It seemed that the reason the cats hadn't flown at them already was because the

Doctor was doing something clever with his sonic screwdriver. He was sweeping it in front of him, creating some sort of barrier or field or something which the cats seemed reluctant to cross. They kept trying, but then would jump back, yowling, as if they'd had a mild electric shock. If the door hadn't been here, she supposed this tactic would have resulted in a tense stalemate, lasting until either the cats returned to normal, the Doctor got cramp or the sonic ran out of juice (if it ever did).

The Doctor glanced over his shoulder and saw the open door. 'Brilliant!' he grinned. 'Aw, I love doors, me. Number one invention of all time. And so versatile. Did you know the outlawing of doors was directly responsible for the fall of the Tymerian Empire? All that extra faff climbing in and out of windows and having to walk up and down stairs 'cos you couldn't use lifts any more meant that nothing ever got done. Productivity dropped, the economy crashed, and all because her Royal Tectrope got her fourth proboscis jammed in a suction door and was made to look a prat. Bonkers. Utterly bonkers.'

By the time he had finished babbling, the three of them were through the door and had hurried down a worn flight of stone steps. They found themselves in a low-ceilinged but sizeable cellar, cold and dank and smelling faintly of apples. The only light came from a fur-coated bulb hanging from six inches of flex in the centre of the ceiling. A long slit of a window, hinged at the top and set at eye-level in the opposite wall, provided the only visible escape route. The green foggy darkness pressing against the glass gave Martha the odd sensation that they were underwater.

The Doctor looked around. 'Norman Bates chic,' he said musingly. 'Like it.'

Above them they could hear the cats mewling and padding about. The Doctor pointed at a large wooden trapdoor set into the stone-flagged floor. 'What's that?'

Etta frowned, obviously irritated by what she saw as an irrelevant question. 'It's a fruit store,' she said. 'Nothing but a big, airtight box in the earth. There's no way out through there, if that's what you're thinking.'

Martha noticed the Doctor purse his lips, noticed too the way his dark, unblinking eyes lingered on the trapdoor for a moment. Then he hurried across to the long, narrow window on the far side of the room.

'Shame about the cats,' he said as he unlatched the window and cautiously lifted it. 'I was getting quite fond of them again after all the friendly ones we met on New Earth. But this lot have blotted the copybook. They've sent cats plummeting right back down my species popularity chart. Not that it's their fault, I suppose.'

Martha glanced at Etta to see how she was taking all this, considering that the old lady was obviously a cat lover. Etta didn't look angry, however, merely worried. Martha could guess what question Etta wanted – but was afraid – to ask, and so she asked it herself. 'Will they stay like that?'

The Doctor was peering through the long letterbox slit of the window, presumably on the lookout for more hell-cats. Wisps of green mist drifted in through the gap like probing, ghostly fingers.

'Nah,' he said dismissively. 'Soon as whoever's put the hex on them realises we've legged it, I expect they'll switch off the old voodoo. Your moggies will be harmless little furballs again by the morning, I should think, Etta. Probably be a bit offish, but blimey, they're cats – who's gonna notice the difference?'

He lifted the window all the way open and pushed it back. 'Right, I think the coast's clear. Come on.'

He levered himself out with no apparent effort, then grabbed Martha's hand and hauled her out just as easily. Not for the first time she was surprised – and impressed – by his wiry strength.

Together the two of them then pulled Etta out of

the window. She was not a slim lady, and it was a narrow gap, but after a bit of oofing on everyone's part they managed it.

Standing in Etta's backyard, mist curling around them, the Doctor suddenly looked a bit awkward.

'Um… sorry for causing you all this bother,' he said to Etta.

She looked sternly at him for a moment, and then her face broke into a smile. 'You know what? I haven't had this much excitement in years.'

The Doctor looked delighted. 'Aw, bless.'

'So what now?' Martha asked.

He puffed out his cheeks. 'Well, I dunno about you, but I'm parched. Back to the hotel for a nice cuppa, I think.'

'Jeez, will you get off my case!' shouted Chris.

He jumped up from the breakfast table, pushing his cereal bowl away, causing milk to slop onto his place mat.

'Hey! Don't talk to your mom like that,' growled Tony Pirelli.

'But she's treating me like a kid,' Chris protested.

'Well, that's probably because you're acting like one,' his dad said.

The boys' mother, Amanda, looked upset. 'I only wanted you to have a proper breakfast,' she said.

'You know I don't like you skipping meals, Chris.'

'But I've told you,' Chris said, 'I'm not hungry.'

'And why *is* that?' his dad asked pointedly.

Chris spread his hands. 'I'm just not. Why does there *have* to be a reason?'

Suddenly Tony Pirelli looked very serious. 'It's not drugs, is it, Chris?'

Chris rolled his eyes. 'Oh, gimme a break.' Then he became aware that *both* his parents were looking at him, their faces grim and anxious. He looked back at them, aghast. 'Man, I don't believe this. No, it's *not* drugs. Drugs are for losers.'

'But you *are* a loser,' muttered Rick, who was obediently eating his Cheerios and had been silent up to now.

'Takes one to know one, runt-features,' Chris said.

'I am *not* having that kind of talk at the meal table,' snapped Tony.

'*He* started it,' Chris protested. 'Why don't you tell *him?*'

'I'm telling both of you,' said their dad.

'Sorry, Dad,' said Rick demurely.

Chris pulled a disgusted face. 'I'm outta here.'

'Not before cleaning up this mess you're not,' his dad said, indicating the spilled milk on the table.

Chris tutted, grabbed a wad of kitchen paper and

used it to mop up the milk, then dumped the wet paper in the trash. 'Now can I go?'

'That depends where you're going to,' his dad said.

'Nowhere,' said Chris, then seeing the thunderous expression forming on his dad's face he sullenly conceded, 'Brad's.'

'And will you and Brad be coming along to help us set up the Halloween Carnival?' Tony asked pointedly.

Chris shrugged. 'Dunno.'

'It would be nice if you did, Chris,' his mom said. 'I'm sure your dad and the rest of the Halloween Committee would be grateful for all the help they can get.'

'Yeah, whatever,' Chris said and slouched towards the door. Then he sighed and turned back. 'Maybe we'll come along later,' he muttered.

'Don't bust a gut,' his dad said.

As he tromped down the street, Chris felt bad. He hadn't *liked* running out on his parents, but he was still scared after what had happened in the night, and being scared had made him too angry to talk. He just needed to be on his own for a while to think about what he'd seen and what, if anything, he was going to do about it. He turned out of his street and was heading off down the road towards town, when a voice behind him shouted, 'Hiya!'

Chris turned. Jogging towards him through the mist was a skinny man wearing a tight suit and a long brown coat, an inane grin on his face.

Oh great, Chris thought, *this is all I need.* Scowling he said, 'Have I got a sign above my head or something?'

The man stopped and scrutinised him so intently that Chris felt as if his thoughts were being read. Then the guy glanced above Chris's head. 'Er... no,' he said. 'Should you have?'

Chris sighed. 'Whatever you're selling, I'm not interested. What is this? Hassle Chris Day or something?'

'There you go,' said the man. 'Knew I was right.'

'About what?'

'About you being him.'

'Who?'

Under his breath the man said, 'Blimey, it's true what they say about teenagers.' Slowly he enunciated, 'You. Chris. Pirelli. Yes?'

Chris scowled. 'So what if I am?'

With a pleasant smile the man said, 'Tell you what, Chrissy boy, let's just skip all the teenage angsty stuff. We'll take it as read that you've got *issues*, that no one understands you and that you're confused about your sexuality.'

'I'm not—' Chris began, but the man shushed him.

'Because otherwise this planet will be in flames by the time we finally finish this conversation, and if anyone tries to blame me for not saving it like I usually do, I'll just point the finger and say, "It was his fault – Mr Awkward Pants here".'

Chris stared at the smiling man and noticed again how dark and weird his eyes were. Maybe he was just a loon, though Chris couldn't help thinking there was more to him than that. He couldn't help thinking, in fact, that the guy was not just smart, but that somehow he saw *everything*.

'Who *are* you?' he asked.

'I'm the Doctor,' the man said.

'The Doctor?' repeated Chris heavily.

'Oh, yes,' said the man, as if he expected Chris to be impressed.

'Ohhh-kay. So what's that supposed to mean? Is it, like, some online geek-boy name or something?'

The man blinked, swallowed. For a moment he looked uncertain how to respond. Then he said, 'Anyway, moving swiftly on… Where's the book, Chris?'

'What book?'

Suddenly the guy looked deadly serious. 'I really haven't got time for this.'

'But… but I don't know what you're talking about,' Chris said weakly.

The man stared at him a moment longer – and then the easy smile was back. 'No, you don't, do you? So what's bothering you then?'

Again Chris got the impression that the man could see into his head. 'Nothing,' he said quickly.

'OK,' said the man with a dismissive shrug and turned away. 'See you later.'

Chris stayed silent for maybe three seconds, watching the man – *the Doctor* – saunter along the sidewalk. And then he called, 'What makes you think I've got stuff on my mind?'

The Doctor stopped. Then he pivoted on his heels. His face was grim, but not unsympathetic. Quietly he said, 'Oh, I've seen so much fear in my life, Chris. So many people with so many secrets that they can't or won't or daren't share. And you know what the funny thing is? Most of the time those people don't even know *why* they're keeping their secrets. Maybe they think they won't be believed, or even that people will laugh at them.' He shrugged. 'I dunno. What do *you* think?'

Chris was silent for a moment, then he blurted, 'I saw something!'

'Oh yeah?' said the Doctor casually.

'Last night. I woke up and I looked out of my

window, and… and…'

'And I promise that whatever you tell me, I'll believe you,' the Doctor murmured, and Chris saw in his dark, unblinking eyes that the Doctor was speaking the truth.

So he told his story – about the strange light, and the tree that wasn't a tree, and about how the man who couldn't possibly have been a man (no matter how much Chris had tried to convince himself otherwise) had been swallowed by the earth.

The Doctor's eyes got starier and darker during the telling. And the more Chris talked, the more the Doctor looked as if he was trying to remember something important.

'Tell me what this tall man looked like,' he said, after Chris had described how the figure had sunk into the ground.

'He was the thinnest guy I've ever seen,' Chris said, 'and he had these great big hands with fingers that were, I dunno, maybe a foot and a half long? And a huge head, like… like…' It suddenly dawned on him what the thing's head had reminded him of. 'Like a Halloween pumpkin.'

The Doctor raised his eyebrows as realisation dawned. 'Hervoken,' he said, and he said it in such a way that it made Chris shudder.

Chris licked his lips. He could barely get his voice

above a whispery rasp. 'Pardon me?'

'Hervoken,' the Doctor repeated, then he half-spun round and slapped himself theatrically on the forehead. 'Oh, I *should* have realised! *Why* didn't I realise? What a prawn!'

Bewildered, Chris said, 'Hey, don't beat yourself up about it, man. So what are these…'

'Hervoken,' the Doctor said for the third time. 'They're—' He looked as if he was about to launch into a whirlwind explanation, then suddenly checked himself, as if he had belatedly realised the full extent of Chris's confusion and fear, and had decided that maybe the boy wouldn't be able to handle it. Abruptly he grinned and gave Chris a friendly slap on the upper arm. 'Never you mind, feller. You just keep your head down and leave it to me. I'll sort it.'

'Will you?' Chris said, clearly out of his depth.

'Oh yeah,' said the Doctor with a confident wink. 'Do this sort of thing all the time, me.'

Martha was not a happy bunny. After getting back to the hotel the night before, she had generously offered Etta her bed, half-hoping the Doctor would offer her his in return. It was not that she expected him to declare his undying love for her or anything, but a little old-fashioned chivalry at the end of a long day would not have gone amiss.

Instead he had said goodnight seemingly oblivious to her situation, leaving her to make the best of a small sofa, on which she could only lie down if she brought her knees up to her chest. Even then, she was so tired that that *might* have been bearable, were it not for the fact that Etta's snoring had kept her awake all night. If she hadn't heard it herself, Martha would never have believed it possible that someone could snore even louder than her brother Leo after a few drinks. The noise Etta made was like the braying of a distressed donkey – and what was worse was that it never stopped. It went on and on and on…

In the end Martha shut herself into the bathroom and tried to doze in the bath with a big fluffy towel half-wrapped round her head.

When even *that* didn't work, she got up, grabbed herself a long, hot shower and went off in search of the Doctor and coffee.

But the Doctor's room was locked and he didn't answer her knocks. And when Martha asked Eloise Walsh about him, she was told that he'd headed out, fresh as a daisy, at first light.

'That's if you can even *call* this daylight,' Eloise said mournfully, staring at the thick veil of green mist pressing against the glass-panelled doors of the hotel. 'I've never seen anything like it, and I've lived in the Falls all my life. Gives me the creeps, I don't mind telling you. Hope it passes in time for the Carnival.'

Martha shrugged. 'Won't it just add to the atmosphere?'

'Hmm,' said Eloise doubtfully. 'It's a tad *too much* atmosphere if y'ask me. After what happened to poor Earl last night, I'm thinking of staying right here this evening – and I haven't missed a Halloween Carnival since I was a little girl.'

'How is Mr Clayton today?' Martha asked.

'That's *Dr* Clayton,' corrected Eloise.

'Sorry. Dr Clayton.'

'He's as comfortable as they can make him, from what I hear. Having to feed him with tubes, though. Poor feller must be scared out of his wits.'

'Yes,' said Martha. 'He must be.'

'So you and this doctor of yours didn't find anything last night?' Eloise asked.

'Not much,' said Martha evasively, 'but we're working on it.'

Eloise gave her a shrewd look and pointed at the ceiling. 'So who's your friend?'

'Ah.' Martha and the Doctor had sneaked Etta into the hotel to avoid convoluted explanations. 'So you know about that then?'

Eloise smiled thinly. 'I may be old, Miss Jones, but I'm not deaf.'

Martha looked suitably abashed. 'Yeah, the snoring *is* a bit of a giveaway, isn't it?'

Eloise said nothing, merely raised an eyebrow. She was evidently waiting for an explanation.

Martha sighed. 'It's Etta Helligan.'

Now Eloise raised *both* eyebrows. 'Etta? Well, in that case, would you care to tell me *why* you brought her back here? You and that doctor friend of yours kidnapping our old people?'

Martha couldn't tell whether Eloise was joking or not. 'We met her when we were out last night,' she said. 'We walked her home, but then we… we heard someone outside her house. A prowler or something. We didn't like the thought of leaving her on her own, so we… brought her back here.' Fearing that Eloise would start picking holes in her rather feeble explanation, she asked quickly, 'Have you any idea which way the Doctor went?'

Eloise shrugged. 'Can't say I have. Guess he just went for a walk to clear his head. Be back soon, I dare say.'

'Yes, I expect so,' said Martha. 'Well… see you.'

'You going for a walk too?'

Martha laughed lightly. 'I need a bit of fresh air. Well…' She glanced dubiously at the green mist beyond the doors '… *Air*, anyway. After last night I feel a bit… you know?' She pointed meaningfully up at the ceiling.

'I hear you,' said Eloise. 'You want me to give Etta a message if she shows her face?'

'Just tell her... I'll be back soon.'

Martha exited the hotel at something of a loss. It would be pointless wandering around town looking for the Doctor, but she certainly couldn't face sitting in her room, going stir crazy, waiting for him to show up. She looked around, and through the murk hanging over the central square she noticed a flashing neon sign. The words were blurry, but she could just make them out: LEO'S DINER.

Leo. Same name as her brother. That *had* to be an omen. As if spotting the sign had prompted it, her stomach rumbled, and she realised she hadn't eaten anything since the chocolate fudge sundae she'd scoffed in Harry Ho's yesterday afternoon.

Right, she decided, breakfast. After the torture of last night's snore-fest she deserved the full works – bacon, sausage, eggs, beans, hash browns, toast, marmalade... and lots and lots of caffeine.

She walked across the street and into the diner. It was warm and smelled of frying bacon and coffee. The mist outside and the condensation on the windows gave her the impression the building was wrapped in green cotton wool. There was music playing in the background: bland American rock by the sort of group who named themselves after where they came from – Boston, Chicago, something like that. The place wasn't very full, possibly because it was early, or because the mist was making people reluctant to leave their homes. Like every other place in Blackwood Falls, the inside of the diner was decorated with the trappings of Halloween – paper ghosts, cardboard witches, glow-in-the-dark skeletons.

Above the counter a row of spiky-furred cats made of black crepe paper reminded Martha of Etta's murderous moggies. She wondered whether the Doctor had gone back to the old lady's house, and decided that if he didn't turn up within the next hour then that was where she would head for.

It wasn't much of a plan, but having one at all made her feel a little better.

'Table for one?' called the grizzled, sweating man cooking food behind the counter.

'Please,' said Martha.

'Sit anywhere you like, sweetheart. We ain't exactly busting at the seams this morning.'

Martha plonked herself in a booth by the window, where she could look out into the street. Not that she could see much. The slowly swirling mist was like a reminder of how tired she was, how sluggishly her thoughts were moving about in her head.

A grinning girl with bright blue eyes and ash-blonde hair appeared at her table and cried chirpily, 'Hi, I'm your waitress this morning and my name's Cindy.'

'Yeah,' muttered Martha under her breath, 'it just *had* to be.'

If Cindy heard Martha's comment she didn't let on. Eager as a cartoon chipmunk she asked, 'What can I get for you this morning?'

Martha gave her order and Cindy went away. Thinking of Leo reminded Martha that she was back on present-day Earth, which meant that she could try giving Tish a ring. She took her mobile out of her pocket and scrolled through her address book until she found her sister's number. She was about to press the Call button when it suddenly occurred to her that for Tish this wouldn't actually *be* the present day.

Martha had got so used to rattling back and forth through the centuries with the Doctor that a few months – or even a year or two – before or after that spring day she had originally stepped aboard the TARDIS seemed neither here nor there to her. But calling Tish might change all that, might prove totally disastrous, in fact. What if, for instance, this was a few months into Martha's future (and she was ashamed to say she was only *assuming* this was 2008;

she hadn't actually *checked*) and she called home only to find that something terrible had happened? Or what if, when she rang Tish, her future (or past) self was actually *there* with her sister in the room, and Tish was so freaked out by the experience that it led to… to what?

The Doctor had once told Martha how the same person from different time lines should never come into contact with themselves because it would unravel the web of time or something. She had never really thought about that until now, but all at once she realised how tricky and complicated and dangerous the consequences of time travel could be. Not because of the monsters you might meet along the way, but because of what you yourself, with an act of thoughtlessness, might unwittingly set in motion.

With a shudder, she switched her phone off and put it back in her pocket. Then, as she waited for her food, she thought about how the Doctor must have had to think about this stuff all the time for hundreds of years, and of how brilliant and special and lonely he was. And thinking about *that* gave Martha a renewed tingle not simply of excitement but of sheer, unadulterated joy. It gave her a sense, not for the first time, of how incredibly privileged she was to be travelling with him – of how, in fact, regardless of the sleepless nights and the frequent terror and the almost incessant bumps and bruises, she was the luckiest girl alive.

Deep beneath the earth the Hervoken were communicating.

Theirs was an ancient language, subtle, instinctive and complex. They conveyed meaning not through conventional speech, but via thoughts, feelings, symbols, incantations. To a human being, they might have appeared to be praying, or casting spells, or twitching involuntarily, or at times simply waiting, perhaps even sleeping as they drifted like phantoms on the air. But in truth they were doing none of these things. They were conveying information, formulating a plan.

They knew – through a mysterious fact-gathering process of their own that humans might (only partly correctly) have labelled mind-reading or remote perception or even witchcraft – that the man with the blue energy was a danger to them, and that he had an emotional link to the girl who accompanied him.

And they knew too that the girl was currently alone.

And vulnerable…

* * *

Martha was halfway through her mega fry-up when the hairs started prickling on the backs of her arms. She looked out at the street. Was the mist suddenly thicker and darker? She had been able to see the cars parked by the kerb pretty clearly before, but now they were hazy blocks of dimness. And the vague outline of the buildings across the square had disappeared completely, to be replaced by an almost solid bank of mist that was deepening to the murky green of over-ripe olives.

All at once her breakfast didn't seem so appetising. Because now, as well as the hairs on her arms, Martha felt the hairs on the back of her neck prickling too. Plus her stomach was starting to churn with nerves. She tried to tell herself there was nothing to be afraid of, nothing concrete, nothing she couldn't rise above. Like the Doctor had said, it was just alien chemicals, or psychic oojamaflips, or whatever it was they put in the mist, that were making her feel this way.

Determined to return to her breakfast – even though her appetite had almost completely gone by now – Martha suddenly realised the music that had been playing in the diner had stopped. Tearing her gaze away from the scene outside the window, she turned her head – and gasped.

The room was full of mist! It was suffusing the place with an eerie gloom, obscuring the counter, the surrounding tables, the Halloween decorations, Martha's fellow diners…

She jumped to her feet, her heart thumping hard. It was difficult to tell where the mist was coming from. It seemed to be everywhere and nowhere. It seemed simply to be *there*, filling the room. And it seemed to be deepening even as she looked, turning solid objects into murky blobs, transforming day into night.

Martha felt suddenly alone in the dank silence. Alone, isolated, removed from reality.

'Hello?' she called. 'Anyone around?' She was alarmed at how flat and muffled her voice sounded, how the marshy mist seemed to swallow it.

Suddenly sensing a presence behind her, feeling cold breath on the nape of her neck, she spun round…

There was no one there.

'Hello?' she called again, annoyed at the rising panic in her own voice. 'Will someone please answer me?'

Once again the mist stifled and seemed to gulp down her words. And once again there was no reply.

Right, Martha thought. *Right*. What would the Doctor do? What would he do if he *didn't* have his sonic screwdriver?

He'd make for the door, that's what. He'd try to find out what was going on.

She slid out of the booth and started walking in what she thought was the direction of the door. The mist was so thick now it was like being blind. She could feel it on her skin, like the cobweb-caress of ghostly fingers. It was hard not to get disorientated. Even though she knew the door couldn't be far away, she couldn't help but think she was heading out into a wilderness, a limbo, a nothing-place.

A place where she might get lost and wander forever…

Despite the cold she was sweating. And her heart was still bashing away in her chest. *Calm down*, she told herself. *Don't panic. You're in the diner, that's all. Anything else is just your imagination.*

'I know what you're doing,' she said, trying to sound as if she wasn't affected in the slightest. 'I know what you're doing and it won't work on me. I've seen stuff you wouldn't believe. If you think a bit of mist is going to scare me, then you're very much mis—'

A figure loomed out of the murk. Martha had to use all her willpower to stop herself crying out. Mist drifted over the figure and then spun away, making her think of a present being unwrapped. She leaned forward and saw that it was Cindy. The waitress was standing still as a statue, her eyes wide and glassy, her mouth half-open. She didn't react when Martha touched her shoulder. She didn't even appear to be breathing.

'Cindy?' Martha said. 'Can you hear me?'

The girl didn't respond. Just continued to stare vacantly into space.

Like a standing corpse.

Martha shuddered and moved on.

A couple who had been having breakfast in a booth nearer to the door were similarly affected. The woman was holding a fork with a piece of waffle jammed onto the end of it. Her husband had his right hand curled around a mug of cooling coffee. Both were gazing into space as if they were catatonic with shock.

Was everyone in the diner like this, she wondered. Hypnotised or paralysed or whatever. Was everyone in *town* like this? But why not her? And what about the Doctor?

As if in answer to her question, Martha suddenly realised that she could see someone moving about in the gloom ahead.

'Doctor?' she called. 'Is that you?'

If it was, he was not only moving slowly, but also remaining silent.

Perhaps he can't hear me, she thought. *Perhaps the mist*

is so *thick that he literally can't hear my voice.*

'Doctor?' she shouted again, and the figure drifted closer.

Yes, she thought, *it is him. Or someone tall and thin, at any rate.*

But as the figure came closer still, Martha felt a crawling sense of unease. This wasn't the Doctor. This was a giant, like someone on stilts. And this person wasn't just thin, but *emaciated,* skinny as a rake. And there was something wrong with the person's head. It was too big, too wide, like… like…

Then the figure stepped forward, out of the gloom, and Martha saw it clearly for the first time.

'Oh my…' she breathed and backed away. The creature fixed her with its black, beady eyes. It opened its vast zigzag mouth in its great squashy head, and she saw rows and rows of serrated, shark-like teeth.

She backed into a table, which scraped a few inches across the floor. Cutlery rattled; a ketchup bottle fell over with a thump.

The creature raised a hand which was almost as long as Martha's entire arm. Its taloned fingers moved slowly, clicking like bones as they did so. It made a sound, a breathy, high-pitched sound, something between a sigh, a murmur and a giggle. Then it extended a long, spiny finger and seemed to draw something in the air in front of Martha's face…

… And suddenly she couldn't move!

Every muscle in her body seemed frozen. It was like being tightly bound with strong, invisible rope.

Martha could only stand there, horrified, as the grinning thing reached out for her.

SEVEN

'Here kitty, kitty,' called the Doctor warily, pushing open Etta's front door a few inches and poking his head round the gap.

In a slightly guilty way he was feeling pleased with himself. Unable to use his sonic screwdriver for fear of alerting the Hervoken to his presence, he had gained access to Etta's house with nothing more than a bit of wire and his Alpha Centauri Table Tennis Club membership card. His house-breaking skills were a bit rusty, but he'd managed to get the door open in just under seven seconds. Now all he had to do was get past the army of vicious hell-cats and he was laughing.

Although he had confidently told Etta that the cats would be back to normal this morning, the Doctor had no way of knowing whether that was actually true, beyond doing what he was doing now. If screaming balls of fur with glowing green eyes suddenly came flying at him from all directions, he'd conclude that he'd been wrong and leg it out of there.

He looked left and right and even above his head, but all seemed quiet. 'Ah, K-9,' he murmured, 'where are you when I need you?'

Then a grey cat slunk through the partly open kitchen door at the end of the corridor beside the central staircase and came padding towards him. The Doctor scrutinised it as it approached. It had that serenely disdainful catty swagger about it, and its eyes, though green, were not glowing.

The Doctor stepped into the house and pushed the door closed behind him. Still watchful, he crouched down and let the cat come to him. It slunk around his ankles a couple of times, then rubbed its face against his knee. He picked it up.

'All right are you now?' he murmured, examining it. He stroked it and it began to purr. 'Word of advice,' he said. 'If you ever get invited to a fancy dress party, don't go as a nun.'

He put the cat down and it sauntered away. Still looking around, the Doctor crossed to the wooden door in the panelling that led to the cellar. He could feel the energy in the air with every step he took.

It tingled in his skin, vibrated in his nerve endings. Although she didn't know it, Etta and her family had been living slap-bang on top of a vast source of alien power for the past couple of hundred years. It was a bit like living on the summit of a simmering volcano. It had been dormant for the most part, but now it was powering up, getting ready to tear a great big hole out of the planet.

Pulling open the wooden door, the Doctor went down into the cellar. He crossed straight to the trapdoor he had asked Etta about last night and tugged it open. A sour-sweet smell wafted up at him, together with a surge of energy so strong it made his flesh tighten, his eyes water and his hair stand up in punky spikes.

'Whoo, talk about overdoing it with the aftershave,' he said, and backed away, rubbing his face vigorously with his hands, running his tongue over his itchy teeth.

When the energy had dispersed a little, he approached the open trapdoor again. Beneath it, just as Etta had said, was a square storage space, about chest-height, lined in sheets of metal to make it impervious to rodents and other pests. It was empty now, aside from the lingering ghosts of long-ago fruit harvests. The Doctor jumped down into the hole, his feet clanging on the metal floor.

He had a theory, and he wanted to test it out. He knew, or at least suspected, that the Hervoken could not have survived all this time, even in their dormant state, without help. He ran his hands over the metal walls of the storage chamber, probing for gaps, searching for a dodgy hinge, a hidden catch, anything. It didn't take him long to find it, a loose rivet at the top of the right-hand wall. He pressed it confidently – and nothing happened. Nonplussed, he tried twiddling it, and a metal door about a metre square swung open to the side of him.

'Now *that's* what I call a cat flap,' he muttered, and rummaged in his pocket until he found a pencil-torch. He turned it on and shone it into the darkness beyond the door. The light revealed a narrow tunnel, the walls roughly clad in rotting timber.

'Ready or not, here I come,' he said, and clamping the torch between his teeth he crawled inside.

The walls were writhing around her. The ceiling was undulating above her head. Even the floor was rippling beneath her feet. Martha's entire surroundings were made up of black roots or vines, which were constantly on the move, twisting and intertwining like a chamber of snakes. She might have thought they *were* snakes if it wasn't for the fact that green light was pulsing and flickering through them, bathing the place in a dim, toxic glow. Indeed, the only thing that *wasn't* moving in the hellish environment was Martha herself. She was immobile, her muscles locked into place, able to do nothing but think and observe.

She was trying to stay calm, to behave as the Doctor would behave, to look around with interest and curiosity. She was trying to overcome the fact that she was terrified out of her wits, trying to tell herself that the reason she kept stepping back into the TARDIS was precisely so that she could have experiences like this.

I mean, she thought, *here I am in an alien... lair? Base? Anyway, here I am. And I'm surrounded by giant, skinny pumpkin-men. I mean, how amazing is that?*

The pumpkin-men, she knew, were called Hervoken. She knew that because she could understand their language, even though it was composed not of traditional speech, but of a complicated fusion of chants and movements and little rituals. Thanks to the TARDIS she understood the Hervoken's body language, their facial expressions, even their silences. She knew that they were wary of the Doctor, that they considered him dangerous simply because of the technology they had detected him using. She was aware too that they knew he was different to the other inhabitants of the planet because he had… she wasn't sure exactly what word they used here, either because there wasn't an English equivalent of it or because their language was *so* alien and ancient that even the TARDIS struggled to translate it, but the closest she could get to it was 'aura'. They considered the Doctor dangerous because he had an *aura* about him.

When Martha heard the Hervoken 'talking' about *her*, she tried not to look alarmed or interested, tried not to let on that she knew what they were saying. They talked about her as a 'hostage', as a 'bargaining tool'. She knew that they had taken her in the belief that the Doctor wouldn't move against them whilst they had her in their clutches.

Wrong, she thought. OK, so she knew the Doctor would back off if they threatened to kill her, but that didn't mean he'd sit on his bum and do nothing. All the time she was here he'd be beavering away somewhere, thinking of ways to stop them if they needed stopping, or help them if they needed helping.

Martha was trying to store it all up, trying to remember all the things she had seen and heard in case it proved useful later. She had learned that the Hervoken's power reserves were low, and that even with the 'Necris', which was the book on top of the plinth-thing in the centre of the room, there was now barely enough left to channel their psychic energy. Paralysing all the people in the diner while they had grabbed her had taken a lot out of them, and they needed a temporary power boost to keep things ticking over. Without it the – she translated it as 'sky-heart', though took it to mean the place they were currently standing in – the 'sky-heart' would slip back into dormancy, forcing the Hervoken once again into hibernation.

Works for me, she thought, though in truth she knew that that would only be pushing the problem underground for future generations to cope with, kind of like burying nuclear waste. She watched as the Hervoken gathered around the Necris and began to chant, their soft, childlike voices making Martha feel woozy, although not in a good way. Theirs was a lullaby that promised terrible nightmares rather than sweet dreams.

The Hervoken sketched symbols in the air with their hideous fingers. The one she took to be their leader simply because he (or was it a she? Martha had no idea) seemed to initiate everything, produced some kind of powder or dust, apparently from nowhere, and scattered it in a ritualistic pattern.

One of the Hervoken stepped forward and placed a hand on the Necris. Instantly all the bubbles of green light that flickered and flashed intermittently among the writhing vines seemed to rush towards the centre of the chamber, to gather at the base of the plinth and flow upwards. The Hervoken with its hand on the book became bathed in green light. It opened its wide mouth and hissed, reminding Martha oddly of a man stepping into a warm shower after a hard day's work. The light enveloped the Hervoken completely, filling its deep-set eyes and the black, jagged crack of its mouth, until it looked more like a Halloween pumpkin than ever.

And then, fizzing like a soluble Aspirin dropped into water, the alien faded away.

In the tunnel the Doctor felt the hairs rising on the nape of his neck. He held out his left hand and saw the hairs stiffening, standing to attention. He sucked his index finger and held it up, as though to gauge the wind direction.

'Frying tonight,' he murmured. 'Definitely on the right track.'

He crawled on.

Panting and sweating, Rick, Scott and Thad were helping to carry lengths of timber and unwanted items of furniture from the big woodshed on the edge of Juniper Park to the growing pyramid of flammable material which would form the Pumpkin

Man's funeral pyre at the climax of tonight's festivities. The fire was a Blackwood Falls Halloween tradition. Nobody knew who had started it or where it had come from, but every year the townsfolk made a Pumpkin Man out of paper and straw, sticks and old clothes, which was placed on top of the fire and burned to ashes. Rick knew the British had something along the same lines, where they burned an effigy of some guy who had tried to blow up their Parliament. He didn't think that happened on Halloween night, though, and he didn't think the British burned their guy for the same reason the townsfolk of Blackwood Falls burned their Pumpkin Man, which was to ward off evil spirits and keep the town safe for another year.

It was a long walk from the woodshed to the bonfire site – all the way past the bleachers and the baseball diamond, the Carnival marquee and the stalls set up either side of it in a kind of giant horseshoe shape – and by 10.30am the boys were ready for a rest.

Rick's dad, who was helping to build the bonfire itself, dressed in construction worker's hardhat and canvas gloves, put his hand in his pocket and pulled out a ten dollar note.

'Good work, boys. I think you've earned yourselves a soda,' he said, handing Rick the money.

The boys thanked him. 'Is it OK if we have a look round before we come back, Dad, see how things are shaping up?' Rick asked.

'Yeah, we need to pace ourselves, Mr Pirelli,' said Scott, palming sweat from his shiny red face, 'otherwise we'll be beat by lunchtime.'

Tony Pirelli grinned. 'Sure, guys. Take a break. Come back when you're ready. This isn't an obligation, you know. *Any* help you give will be gratefully received.'

'Oh, we'll be back, Dad. We like helping, don't we, guys? It's all part of the fun.'

Scott and Thad both nodded.

'I wish your brother felt the same way,' Mr Pirelli said with a frown.

'Maybe Chris'll be along later,' said Rick.

'Yeah,' said Mr Pirelli flatly, 'maybe.'

The boys wandered back through the mist-shrouded park, eager to check out how the other preparations were coming along. The red and white striped marquee had been erected a couple of days previously, as had the Halloween Carnival banner over the park entrance.

The rides were being set up over on the football field, but most of the current action was focused on the stalls radiating out from the central marquee. Each stall fell roughly into one of three categories

– games, food and stuff to buy. The games were fun but simple affairs – coconut shy, tombola, hook-a-duck; the food comprised everything from hot dogs and fries to candy and cakes; and the stuff to buy was mainly second-hand or home-made: jewellery, books, T-shirts, and little knick-knacks that you'd pick up because they were cute, then throw in the trash a week later.

Every year since they had been old enough to help – and Rick's dad, who was on the town's Activities Committee had first brought Rick and his friends along to the showground when they were six or seven years old – the boys had 'walked the walk' on the morning before the Carnival itself, drinking in the atmosphere, revelling in the anticipation of what was to come.

This year, though, was kind of different. Maybe it was the mist, but there was a flatness in the air, a sense of… not doom exactly, but foreboding. People seemed edgy, preoccupied. There was none of the usual laughing and joking and good-hearted banter.

'Do you think it's true what that Doctor guy said?' Scott asked cautiously.

Rick and Thad both looked at him. This was the first time any of them had referred to the events of yesterday afternoon, when the weird guy who'd turned up in Harry Ho's had accompanied them to Rick's house, only to find the book had gone missing from under Rick's bed. It wasn't, Rick told himself, because they'd been *avoiding* talking about it, it was just that they hadn't had the chance.

Now, though, he found his stomach tightening and his shoulders hunching, almost as if he was drawing in his defences. 'About what?' he all but snapped.

Scott glanced around. He lowered his voice as if afraid of being overheard. 'About the mist? About how it's our fault?'

'I don't see how it *can* be,' said Thad a little whinily.

'He said it came up out of the hole we dug,' said Scott, 'like poisonous gas or something.'

'Who says it's poisonous?' said Rick quickly.

'Well, OK, not poisonous then, but… I dunno. It's not *natural*, is it?'

Rick scowled. 'Yeah, well… what makes this Doctor guy such an expert? I mean, we don't know anything about him. He seemed pretty crazy to me.'

'I thought he was kind of cool,' said Thad quietly.

Rick made an exasperated sound. 'You think *Einstein*'s cool.'

'Well, he is,' said Thad.

Scott shook his head sadly, as if there was no hope.

'Look,' said Rick, 'the guy wanted the book and the book wasn't there, which pretty much means that this whole situation is out of our hands now, right?'

He thought briefly about his nightmare (which had somehow seemed *more* than a nightmare) last night, in which the eyes of his Halloween costume had seemed to glow. But he quickly clamped down on the memory.

Scott looked as if he wanted to say something more, but was reluctant to do so. Rick wasn't about to encourage him, but then Thad said, 'What's wrong, Scott? You look as though you need the toilet real bad.'

'I heard some weird stuff happened last night,' Scott blurted.

'Like what?' said Thad.

'Something happened to Dr Clayton. He had some kind of accident. Something no one seems to want to talk about.'

'Oh yeah?' said Rick. 'And who told you this?'

'I heard my mom talking to Mrs Fisher on the phone. And she heard it from Mrs Walsh. Apparently, Mrs Walsh says that whatever happened to old man Clayton, she'd never seen anything like it.'

'Is he dead?' Thad asked, eyes wide behind his spectacles.

'No, he's in hospital. But no one's allowed to visit him.'

'Aw, he probably just got drunk and fell over and cracked his stupid head open,' Rick said, then immediately regretted his use of the word 'stupid'. Dr Clayton wasn't stupid, he was just sad. Tragic even.

'From what my mom was saying, it was freakier than that,' said Scott.

'Yeah? Well, sometimes dumb rumours get spread around that aren't true. Come on, guys, let's get that soda.'

The boys trooped past the stalls to the park entrance, each of them silent now. Rick was scowling, out of sorts. Not even the thought of the fun they'd be having that evening could cheer him up. In fact, there was a part of him that wished the Halloween Carnival wasn't happening at all, a part of him that would be glad when it was over. They passed beneath the banner at the entrance. A voice hailed them as they did so: 'Hey, you guys, how's it going?'

Rick jumped, at first unable to identify the source of the voice. Then he realised it was coming from above his head and looked up. One of his neighbours,

Mr Everson, was at the top of a tall ladder, fixing some coloured lights to one of the wooden stanchions, across which the banner had been hung. Mr Everson was a big, bearded guy with long straggly hair, which flowed from beneath the brim of his Boston Red Sox cap. He had a hammer in his right hand and a bunch of six-inch nails sticking out of the breast pocket of his green and black lumberjack shirt.

'Hey, Mr Everson,' Rick shouted. 'We're just going for a soda. You want one?'

'Mighty kind of you, Rick, but I got myself a flask of coffee right there in my bag. So, you boys going trick-or-treating tonight?'

'Yes, sir,' said Scott.

'I guess,' said Rick with rather less enthusiasm.

'Well, you have a good time, y'hear?'

'Yes, sir, we will,' said Rick. 'See you later, Mr Everson.'

The boys turned out of the gate and set off up the road towards old Mr Mackeson's corner store. Mr Mackeson had a dog that used to scare them with its barking when they were younger, but which was a blind, mangy old thing now, barely able to raise a growl.

They had gone no more than twenty metres when they heard a cry from behind them, abruptly cut off, and then the clatter of something falling to the ground. The three of them glanced at each other in alarm.

'That's Mr Everson,' said Rick.

They ran back in the direction they had come. Although they had only walked a little way up the road, the park entrance had already been swallowed by mist. After a few seconds, however, it came into sight, and Rick scanned the ground, expecting to see his neighbour lying injured or unconscious, having fallen off his ladder.

But there was no sign of him. Rick looked up. He wasn't at the top of his ladder either.

'Where's he gone?' asked Scott pointlessly.

'Dunno, but his hammer's there,' said Thad, pointing. 'That must have been what we heard hitting the ground.'

Rick approached the hammer, mystified. Questions ran through his mind. If Mr Everson had fallen, why wasn't he here? If it was only his hammer he'd dropped, where was he now? Why hadn't he picked it up? Even more disturbingly, why had he cried out? And why had the cry been suddenly cut off?

He bent and reached for the hammer – and suddenly, as though alerted by his proximity, spidery threads of green light began to flicker around it, to dance up and down its handle and its metal head.

Rick snatched his hand back, alarmed.

'Whoa!' cried Thad. 'Did you see that?'

Scott's eyes were wide with fear. 'Where is Mr Everson? What's happened to him?'

'I think he's been taken,' said Rick.

'Taken? Taken where?' bleated Scott.

But Rick could only look at him with eyes as fearful as Scott's own and shake his head.

The Hervoken that had disappeared was gone for maybe thirty seconds. When it returned, unfolding from a bilious mass of glowing energy which formed in the air, it was not alone. It was accompanied by a bearded man in a baseball cap and lumberjack shirt, whose mouth was open in shock. The man staggered forward, as if shoved from behind, his head turning rapidly from left to right as he looked around him. He spotted Martha, and goggled at her in bewilderment. She was only sorry she couldn't smile or wave or offer him any words of encouragement. Then the man seemed to register his surroundings and Martha saw the shock turn to fear on his face. It was several seconds, however, as though his mind could only handle one thing at a time, before he seemed to notice the Hervoken themselves.

As soon as he did he yelled out in panic and broke into a stumbling run. He clearly wasn't running with any particular goal in mind, but merely following his instincts and trying to get as far away as possible from the creatures around him. He had taken only a few steps when the Hervoken leader reached out a hand and sketched an intricate shape in the air. Instantly the man froze in mid-step, held immobile. Martha saw the utter panic on his face and tried to convey calmness to him with her eyes, but he didn't even look at her.

The Hervoken leader then drew a circular shape in the air before quickly spreading its taloned fingers in what Martha thought of as the kind of gesture that might be used to describe an explosion. Instantly, threads of green energy looped around the man like shimmering coils of rope and propelled him towards the wall of writhing black roots. To Martha's horror, the wall suddenly opened up like a huge, toothless mouth and the man disappeared, screaming, inside. The hole closed behind him, like that of a massive predator closing on its prey, and his scream was abruptly cut off. A moment later Martha heard another sound, a sound that – though she remained upright – turned her legs to jelly.

It was the splintering crunch of bones.

EIGHT

It wasn't long before the tunnel widened out, enabling the Doctor to stand up. He brushed off the knees of his suit, stretched, and spat out the torch, which he caught neatly in his right hand. He was intrigued to see that, beyond the spot where the rotting timber cladding petered out, the walls, floor and ceiling appeared to be moving. He shone his torch on them and strolled over. Thick, black vines, knobbly and glistening, were writhing over and around and in between one another, thousands and thousands of them.

He poked one and it did two things: it flashed briefly with green light and it gave him a mild electric shock.

'Ow,' he said, and waggled his fingers in the air to get the tingly numbness out of them. He put on his black-rimmed spectacles and examined the vines more closely.

'Kinetic binary fusion,' he murmured with a soppy grin. 'That's beautiful. In an icky, slimy, creepy sort of way.'

He was about to move on when something happened. First the vines clenched; then they shuddered; then they began to move more quickly. At the same time a renewed surge of green light rippled through them, bathing the tunnel in a virescent shimmer.

At first the Doctor thought an alarm had been triggered by his prodding the vine. Then he realised what it really was.

'Someone's happy,' he said. 'Had a little feed, have you? A little power boost?'

The Doctor's face was grim. Although he had never personally encountered the Hervoken before, he knew exactly what sort of power they used.

He pressed on, and eventually the tunnel branched out into two tunnels, then three, and then into chambers which sometimes contained as many as six burrow-like exits. He marvelled at the whole tentacular, subterranean system, imagined it stretching the length and breadth of Blackwood Falls, with all the townspeople living on top of it, like tiny parasites on the back of a giant crab. The deeper he went, the less featureless the tunnels became. Nodular growths bulged in greater profusion from the walls and floors, some of which looked like boulders, whilst others resembled twisted columns or lightning-blasted trees.

Green light was bubbling and burping and flickering all around him now, though even with the boost it had just received the Doctor could tell that the system was barely ticking over. Although he didn't know his way about, he was following his nose, or rather his tingling skin and itchy teeth, to what he guessed would be the control centre. Etta's house might be drenched in residual energy because it was bang on top of the bit of Hervoken technology closest to the surface, but the real power, the real heart of the place, lay much deeper.

It didn't surprise him that he didn't encounter any Hervoken on his journey. Theirs was a species based more on the cerebral than the physical. Unlike humans, they didn't need to scurry about from one place to another; they didn't need to see and smell and touch and taste and feel everything they came into contact with. They were not an emotionless race, but they were a profoundly insular one, and therefore callous, oblivious to the desires and feelings of others. If they needed to do something that was necessary to their well-being, then they'd do it, no matter who or what might suffer in the process. Even in ancient times, before they were banished, the Hervoken had lived in a different realm, with different values and concerns to most of the rest of the universe.

It took the Doctor about fifteen minutes to reach the central chamber. As soon as he felt he was getting close, he switched off his torch and put it in his pocket. His teeth were itching unbearably now and he was trying to ignore them. His hair was standing straight up on his head and his skin was sensitive to the touch. The tunnel he was currently walking along was bathed in light that pulsed greener and brighter than anything he had encountered so far. The light came from a vast arched opening at the far end. He crept up to the arch and peeked around the corner.

He saw a huge space, not quite cathedral-like, but not far off. There was lots of 'equipment' in here, though dominant among it was a central dais, attached to the walls on either side by loops of sinewy black vine, and topped by a kind of claw-like tangle of roots. In the middle of the roots nestled what the Doctor guessed was the book that Rick and his friends had dug out from the earth at the base of the tree. Over on the right, standing so motionless that he knew she'd been immobilised, was Martha, looking a bit stressed, but not too worse for wear.

He took a few moments to observe and admire the Hervoken, drifting dreamily about the place like vast, spindly wraiths. They were magnificent creatures, he thought. Striking and enigmatic.

Crouching low, he slipped into the chamber and behind a big bulbous black thing growing out of the floor. Although the black thing looked like nothing but a whacking great pile of congealed dung, the Doctor knew it was actually a very sensitive piece of equipment, and he was careful not to touch it. He waited patiently for his moment, then slipped from the 'dung heap' across to another black thing that looked like a sort of half-melted bouncy castle. From here he was directly opposite where Martha was standing. He waited until all the Hervoken were facing away from him and then he rose up from behind his hiding place and gave her a little wave.

She spotted him immediately and he saw her eyes widen a fraction. He guessed she couldn't react any more than that, which was probably a good thing. It would pretty much have ruined his element of surprise if the Hervoken had caught her gawping at him.

He grinned and winked, then ducked back out of sight again. He sat for perhaps thirty seconds, thinking hard, and then, as he always did, he came up with an idea. Thinking how glad he was to be an ideas man, even if occasionally they turned out to be rubbish, he rooted in his pockets. Thinking also how glad he was to be a man with well-filled pockets, he eventually found what he was looking for, and held it up with a silent *voila!*

It was a safety pin, one of the big old-fashioned kind. The Doctor unfastened it and, without hesitation, jammed the point into the ball of his thumb. Instantly a thick dark bead of blood welled from his punctured skin. Glancing quickly around, the Doctor scuttled from his hiding place over to the wall and smeared the blood onto the nearest writhing vine. He watched in fascination as the vine glowed green and his blood was absorbed. Then he crawled back to his hiding place and started counting.

He had reached eight when the vine convulsed. The convulsion set off a chain reaction, which radiated outwards in all directions, like ripples on a pond. Within seconds, the entire intricate complex of roots and vines was out of control, thrashing in apparent distress.

And, as the Doctor had guessed (or at least hoped) they would be, the Hervoken were affected too. They were clutching their heads and weaving from side to side, a mournful crooning emanating from their beanpole bodies.

The Doctor scrambled to his feet and peered over the top of the bouncy castle thing. On the other side of the chamber, Martha had realised that the Hervoken influence over her had been broken and that she could move again. She stretched and stamped her feet, then took a hesitant step forward. The Doctor ran across the chamber, dodging in and out of the beleaguered Hervoken, and grabbed her hand.

'What did you do?' she shouted.

'I've given the system a touch of indigestion. My blood's a bit rich for its palate.'

'How long will it last?'

'Not long. We should be making tracks.'

Hand in hand they ran back across the chamber.

'Like the hair by the way,' Martha said. 'Very Sonic the Hedgehog.'

The Doctor grimaced. 'I *was* hoping for more of a Sid Vicious vibe. Hang on a sec.'

Instead of heading straight for the exit, he dragged her over to the dais, on top of which sat the book. The tangle of roots holding it in place were clenching and unclenching involuntarily like a hand or a claw. The Doctor waited until its 'fingers' were fully extended, then he reached in and snatched the book.

'He shoots, he scores,' he cried, brandishing his prize in triumph. 'Now let's skedaddle.'

He grabbed Martha's hand once again and they fled through the writhing corridors.

Abandoned, that was how Etta felt. Abandoned and forgotten.

She'd woken up an hour earlier in a strange bed, wondering where the heck she was. It was only when she sat up and saw the green mist outside that she remembered about the Doctor and Martha and her cats.

She was splashing water on her face within a minute and downstairs within three. Eloise Walsh, perched behind her desk like a giant scrawny crow, arched an eyebrow at her.

'Hear you've made yourself some new friends, Etta,' Eloise said, in such a way that she could only be insinuating something.

'So what if I have?' Etta retorted, puffing herself up.

'So nothing,' Eloise said acidly. 'Just making conversation is all.'

'Hmph,' said Etta. She was about to saunter out without another word when it struck her that her new friends might have left her a note or a message. Deciding that it was worth swallowing just a teaspoon of pride in order to find out, she marched over to the desk and asked.

Eloise smirked at the question and said airily, 'The young lady *did* say something about coming back soon, but that was some while ago. I dare say she's found something more diverting to occupy her time. You know what young people are like.'

'And the Doctor?' asked Etta.

'Oh, he left *hours* ago.'

'Did he?' said Etta curtly. She offered Eloise a grudging thank you and plodded towards the main doors.

'Oh, Etta,' Eloise called after her.

Etta clumped to a halt and turned stiffly. 'Mm-hmm.'

'I hope he didn't manage to gain access to your house.'

'Who?'

'Your prowler from last night. Wasn't that why you were here?'

Etta stared at Eloise for a good twenty seconds, then gave a noncommittal 'Mm' and turned away again. She didn't look back.

All the way home she thought about her cats, and hoped that what the Doctor had told her last night was true and that they would be back to normal this morning. She wondered if she'd seen the last of the spaceman and his young friend, whether the two of them had simply vanished as mysteriously as they had appeared. She hoped not. Despite the fact that she'd had to run for her life twice last night, thus exerting her old body more than was probably good for her, she couldn't remember when she had last felt more alive! Men from space, creatures made of leaves, possessed cats… It all made a welcome change from cocoa by the fireside and a book before bedtime.

Even so, she was relieved to find her dear old pets back to normal, just as the Doctor had promised, when she arrived home. If they hadn't been she didn't know what she would have done – run for her life for the third time probably. She put down food and milk for them, and was just about to fix herself a coffee, when she heard a peculiar rumbling sound. Next moment her crockery began rattling on the shelves, prompting several of her cats to abandon their breakfast and dart away with yowls of protest.

What on earth was happening now? Was this the mother ship descending from the heavens? Was the ground about to split asunder and swallow them all whole? She went to the window and looked out. Over her rear fence she could just make out the black tree looming through the mist. She was astonished to see it shuddering and jerking, as if in the grip of a giant hand. She was even more astonished to see sparks of green energy skittering along its branches, and then the ground crack open beneath the pressure of a squirming tangle of thick black roots.

One of the roots, or several, caused her fence to buckle and partially collapse. Etta was still gaping at the black writhing mass, wondering what was going to happen next, when she heard thumping footsteps coming from the direction of her hallway.

She hurried from her kitchen just in time to see her basement door fly open and the Doctor come bounding out. Martha was a few steps behind him, flustered and rosy-cheeked.

Although she had been hoping to see the two of them again, Etta's first response was one of indignation. 'What were you doing in my basement?' she demanded.

'Salt!' the Doctor yelled at her.

'I beg your pardon?'

'Got any salt?'

Taken aback, Etta could only gesture vaguely. 'Yes, it's in the—'

'Kitchen!' the Doctor shouted. 'Course it is!' He bounded past Etta, raced down the corridor and hurtled through the kitchen door.

Martha flashed Etta an apologetic look and ran after him. When Etta entered the kitchen herself, five seconds later, it was to find the Doctor emptying a tub of salt onto her dining table. She watched as he grabbed a handful and rubbed it all over the front cover of the book he was carrying. He gave the spine and the back cover the same treatment, then opened the book seemingly at random and chucked a fistful of salt inside before slamming it shut.

Only then did he allow himself a split second to relax. He expelled a deep breath and said, 'There you go. That'll stop 'em nicking it back until we can get it to the TARDIS.'

'Stop who?' asked Etta.

'Questions are good, but I've only got time to answer relevant ones,' said the Doctor bluntly. 'I'm working to a deadline here.'

'Why is the book so important?' tried Martha.

The Doctor grinned. 'It's their starter motor.'

Etta gave him one of her no-nonsense stares. 'Whatever are you babbling about?'

The Doctor snatched the book off the table and waved it in the air. 'This is their starter motor, and that thing out there,' he pointed towards the back of the house, 'is their spaceship.'

Etta blinked at him. 'Do you mean the tree?'

'The tree,' he confirmed.

'What rot,' she said.

The Doctor stared at her for a moment as if he couldn't believe she had contradicted him. Then he said, 'Do you know, you're right. You're a hundred gazillion per cent right. Because that's *not* their spaceship. That's just the *nose cone* of their spaceship. No, not even that. That's just the tip... tippety... tip bit.' He tapped the end of his nose with his finger and swung to confront Martha. 'What's that bit of your nose called?'

She shrugged. 'The tip.'

'Oh, you're no use,' said the Doctor rudely. 'Call yourself a doctor? Come on!' Abruptly he ran back out of the kitchen, sweeping past Martha and Etta, the book clutched in his hand.

'Where now?' Martha shouted, hurrying after him.

'The TARDIS!' he yelled.

'See you later, Etta,' Martha called back over her shoulder. She slammed the front door after her, and suddenly the house was silent again.

Etta stood in the dusty aftermath of the whirlwind that was the Doctor, and turned to Orlando, who had emerged from hiding now that the 'earthquake' had stopped.

'It's true what they say about the Brits,' she told him. 'Mad as hatters, the lot of them. Even the ones from outer space.'

The TARDIS was encased in a crackling, flickering dome of green energy. The Doctor stopped dead when he saw it, then muttered, 'Right,' and whipped out his sonic. As soon as he turned it on and pointed it at the dome, the crackling intensified. The Doctor adjusted the setting and had another go, but once again the crackling altered, becoming deeper, more sonorous.

'Oh, *now* I'm getting cross,' he grumbled.

'Can't you get through?' asked Martha.

The Doctor tried again, but although the flickering green dome dimmed and brightened intermittently, it remained stubbornly in place.

At last he stepped back and raised his head to the sky. 'I suppose you think you're clever!' he shouted. Then he sighed and grudgingly admitted, 'Which you are. Quite.'

'What's it doing?' asked Martha.

'It's gazumping me,' the Doctor said, and waggled his sonic in the air. 'It keeps anticipating my moves, changing frequency before I do.'

'You mean it's alive?'

'We-ell, not alive exactly, just… a bit brainier than most of the force fields I've met on my travels.' Suddenly he pulled a face. 'Urgh!'

'What's wrong?' Martha asked.

'The Necris is trying to break through the occult shield I created around it.'

She rolled her eyes. 'Hey, this is me you're

talking to, remember. There's no need to tart it all up and make it sound impressive. All you did was cover the book in salt like it was a plate of chips or something.'

'Yeah, but I did it *brilliantly*,' said the Doctor.

Martha smiled. 'So how do you know it's trying to break through then?'

'Well, to use the technical term, it's going all yucky and squirmy. Here, catch.'

He tossed the book to her and she caught it instinctively. Sure enough the cover was rippling, contracting, which made her think of escapologists manipulating their muscles to break free from chains or ropes. 'Yuk,' she said.

'Less of the technobabble,' the Doctor scolded her. 'Long words only confuse people.' He tapped his sonic against his bottom lip, brow furrowed as he thought the situation through. Then he grabbed the book from her again and shouted, 'Come on!'

'Where we going *now*?' she asked as he passed her in a blur of motion.

'Somewhere else,' he called.

'Bet none of your friends have ever been fat, have they?' she shouted, and ran after him.

NINE

'It's just like in the movies,' said Scott.

'Huh?' said Rick.

'You know, those movies where the kids know there's something weird going on, but the adults don't believe them?'

'I bet the Doctor would believe us,' said Thad.

Scott rolled his eyes. 'Yeah, but the Doctor's not here, is he?'

'Well, maybe we should go look for him then,' Thad suggested.

'Oh, *great* idea, brainiac,' said Scott scathingly. 'That shouldn't take too long. There's only about ten million places he could be.'

It was forty-five minutes since Mr Everson's disappearance. By the time Rick had managed to persuade his dad to break away from his work and come look at the hammer, it had long since ceased its weird light show. Rick had warned his dad about touching the thing, but Mr Pirelli had just given him an exasperated look and picked it up anyway. And of course, nothing had happened. The hammer was just a hammer.

'You be sure to give this back to Dwight when you see him,' Mr Pirelli said, and held it out to his son as if making a point.

Rick looked at the hammer as if it was a poisonous snake, but then he stretched out a reluctant hand and took it.

'The thing is, sir,' Scott said hesitantly, 'I don't think we *will* see him.'

Tony Pirelli fixed Scott with a look that made him squirm. 'Really?' he said heavily. 'So *you* think he's vanished into thin air too, huh?'

Scott shrugged, too intimidated to respond.

Thad said, 'We know *something's* happened, Mr Pirelli. We heard him cry out, but when we got here he'd gone.'

'I see. So what's *your* theory, Thad? You think Dwight was maybe snatched by a pterodactyl that slipped through from *The Twilight Zone*?'

His words were steeped in irony. Now it was Thad's turn to fall silent. Shaking his head, Mr Pirelli said, 'You know what I think? I think you guys have got a severe case of the Halloween heebie-jeebies.'

'That's not it, Dad,' protested Rick. 'We *did* hear Mr Everson cry out. And when we got here five seconds later, he'd gone. How do you explain that?'

'Well now, let's see,' said Mr Pirelli, smiling indulgently. 'How's about Dwight was fixing up the lights when he caught his thumb a good one with the hammer? You guys heard him yell out, but by the time you got here he'd scooted off to find himself a band-aid?'

The boys exchanged sceptical looks. 'So what about all the other weird stuff that's been going down?' said Rick.

Mr Pirelli sighed. 'Such as?'

Rick glanced at Scott. 'Dr Clayton for one.'

'What about Dr Clayton?'

'We heard he'd had an accident,' said Rick. 'We heard he was in the hospital and that no one was allowed to visit him.'

Tony Pirelli shrugged. '*If* that's true, then what's weird about it? People have accidents all the time.'

'OK,' said Rick. 'Well, what about this mist? You can't say *this* is normal.'

'It's *unusual*, I'll give you that,' his dad conceded, 'but I'm sure if you asked a weather guy he'd explain it to you like that.' He clicked his fingers.

The boys simply stared at him, unconvinced.

Sighing again, Mr Pirelli said, 'Look, guys, I really haven't got time for this. I have to get back to work. And maybe you should too. Maybe it would help take your mind off things.'

He stomped off, and a few minutes later the boys followed him. Getting back to work *hadn't* helped take their mind off things, however. In fact, the more they talked about Dwight Everson's disappearance the more convinced they became that strange forces were at work.

Scott had just made his remark about there being a million possible places the Doctor could be when Rick said quietly, 'You're not going to believe this, guys.'

Scott and Thad glanced at him, then followed the direction of his gaze. The gangly figure of the Doctor was racing towards them out of the mist, the equally slim but shorter figure of his friend Martha at his heels.

'Hey,' Rick shouted, spotting what the Doctor was holding in his hand, 'you found my book.'

The Doctor and Martha thumped to a stop. Martha was panting, but the Doctor wasn't.

Looking at Rick a little wildly, the Doctor cried, 'I need some iron!'

Bewildered, Rick said, 'Some…?'

'Iron! Iron!' the Doctor shouted. 'Surely you've

heard of it? It's a malleable ductile ferromagnetic metallic element, found mainly in haematite and magnetite. Grappling irons are made out of it, and soldering irons, and... and horses and ages and fists.'

Rick was too flustered by the Doctor's urgency, by the way the man was staring at him, to think clearly. 'What... what kind of iron?' was all he could think of to say.

The Doctor did a double-take. 'Anything! Anything made of iron. A crowbar, a jemmy, an iron... pomegranate. Doesn't matter as long as it's iron.'

Rick suddenly realised that Dwight Everson's hammer was still in his hand. He held it out. 'Well, there's this,' he said.

'Brilliant!' cried the Doctor, as if Rick had performed the most astounding magic trick ever. He snatched the hammer from Rick with one hand and lobbed the book carelessly over his shoulder with the other. Martha stepped forward and caught it.

The Doctor produced what looked to Rick like a thin torch from his coat pocket and turned it on. The torch made a high-pitched warbling noise and a brilliant blue light shone out of the end of it.

'Wow,' Thad breathed as the Doctor used the torch to reshape the iron hammer. Whatever the device really was, it sliced through the dense metal like a sharp knife through a soft cake. The boys watched in awestruck disbelief as the Doctor melted and shaped the chunk of iron, forming it into a band.

'What *is* that thing?' asked Ralph.

'Sonic screwdriver,' said the Doctor absently.

'How does it work?' asked Thad.

'Very well, thanks,' said the Doctor, and reached behind him. 'Martha.'

Martha placed the book into his hand. The Doctor laid it on the iron band, then used his sonic screwdriver to mould the band around it. He made a few minor adjustments, then, when he was happy, sealed the band shut.

Finally he sat back on his heels. 'Try getting out of *that* one,' he said to the book and slipped the sonic back into his pocket.

'So,' Martha said, 'tell us about the Hervoken.'

'The what?' said Rick.

'They're… oh, *so* ancient,' said the Doctor. 'When they're operating at full capacity they have the ability to transform matter, alter perception and shift time.'

'Black magic,' said Thad.

'Just a different kind of science,' said the Doctor. 'They knocked around the universe for centuries, pretty much keeping themselves to themselves, until… ooh, millions of years ago now, they somehow became involved in a war with our old mates, the Carrionites.'

'The Witchy Wars,' Martha said brightly.

The Doctor flashed her a huge grin. 'I *like* that,' he said. 'Aw, I wish my lot had called it that.'

'*Your* lot?' said Rick.

Casually Martha nodded at the Doctor. 'He's an alien.'

There was a beat of stunned silence and then Thad said, 'Cool.'

'So… these Hervoken guys,' said Rick. 'Have they, like, landed here in the Falls? Are they making all this weirdness happen?'

'They didn't *land* here exactly,' said the Doctor. 'They crashed. But not recently.' Briefly he told the boys how the Hervoken ship had come down millennia before, how the majority of it was buried deep in the earth, and how the town had been built around it.

'So the tree's their spaceship?' boggled Scott.

'Well, it's the tip… the apex… the crest… the pinnacle… the peak… the—'

'I think we get the point,' said Martha.

'Hey, how lucky are we to live on top of a whole bunch of aliens?' exclaimed Scott, then withered at the look the Doctor gave him. 'Or not,' he said.

'Luck had nothing to do with it,' said the Doctor. 'Your ancestors were drawn here by a psychic pulse. Nothing too extreme, just a gentle suggestion sent out by the ship. It waited and waited for you lot to get clever enough to help it, then it sought you out and planted instructions in your pliable little brains.' He raised his hands and adopted a ghostly voice: 'Build here, protect us, tend to our needs.'

'By "tend to our needs", do you mean the Hervoken forced the townspeople to...' Martha began, then glanced at the boys, who were all looking at her avidly '... you know?'

The Doctor looked at her in polite incomprehension. Martha rolled her eyes. 'You know,' she said a little more forcefully.

But the Doctor simply pushed out his bottom lip and gave her a blank look. Martha sighed in exasperation and drew a finger swiftly across her throat in the hope that only he would see it. 'You *know*.'

'*Ohh*,' the Doctor cried as realisation dawned, 'offer a human sacrifice, you mean? Nah, don't be daft. The pulse just got the people to create routes to the Hervoken ship, like the one in Etta's cellar, so they could keep things ticking over. Now and again someone was probably chosen to wander about in the corridors so the ship could suck up a few brainwaves. Low maintenance stuff.'

'Oh,' said Martha. 'Well, that doesn't sound too bad.'

'No, it wasn't really. Like I said, they're not exactly life-and-soul types, the Hervoken. They prefer to keep a low profile.'

'So how come they've woken up now?' Rick asked.

'Well, that's down to you lot. Couldn't keep your noses out, could you? Had to dig up old Nelly Necris here.'

He gave them a stern look. The boys looked back, suitably shamefaced. Then the Doctor said airily, 'Though, to be honest, if it hadn't been you it would have been someone else. It was all planned yonks ago – alarm clock set, teasmade primed, eggs on the boil.'

'But why now?' Martha asked.

'Why *not* now?' replied the Doctor. 'I'm guessing it's taken all this time for the ship to repair itself properly and the Necris to work its way to the surface. Plus, knowing the Hervoken, there'll have had to be the right configuration of planets and confluence of whatnots and all that palaver before they could rise again.' He uttered these last two words in a convincingly blood-curdling Vincent Price voice.

'So what do the Hervoken want?' asked Thad. 'Are they here to conquer and enslave humanity?'

'Doubt it,' said the Doctor. 'They probably just want to leave.'

'Well, that's all right then,' said Martha. Then she saw the look on the Doctor's face. 'It's not all right, is it? There's a catch, isn't there?'

'A bit of a one,' the Doctor conceded, waggling his head from side to side.

'Go on then,' sighed Martha. 'Tell us the worst.'

Apologetically the Doctor said, 'Thing is, to take off, the Hervoken ship needs…?' He looked at the boys and raised his eyebrows.

'Fuel?' said Thad.

'Correctamundo!' the Doctor replied, before grimacing. 'Oh, I promised myself I'd never say that again.' He shook his head. 'So yeah, their ship needs fuel. But the trouble is, the fuel it uses—'

'Oh no,' Martha said. 'You're not going to say what I think you're going to say, are you?'

'Depends what you think I'm going to say,' replied the Doctor.

'It's people, isn't it?' said Martha. 'They use people as fuel.'

Again that waggle of the head. 'We-ell… yes and no. To be specific, they use negative emotional energy – terror, pain, distress, that kind of thing

– contained within the raw matter of blood, bone, brain and sinew. It's not very nice, but at least it's environmentally friendly.'

'I think I'm gonna puke,' said Scott.

'How much of this "raw material" will they need?' asked Martha.

'A lot,' said the Doctor, and his words suddenly seemed to ring ominously.

'And when you say a lot you mean…?'

'Oh… round about the population of a small town like this, I'd say.'

'Great,' said Martha. Then she thought of something and nudged the Necris with her foot. 'But we've got their starter motor. Won't that scupper their plans?'

The Doctor wrinkled his nose. 'Oh, I wish I could say yes. But us having the Necris won't stop them fuelling up. They'll be planning something. Something major.'

'What sort of something?' asked Rick.

'Great big cull, I should think. Night of the Long Knives, death and disaster on a massive scale, you know the kind of thing. And I'll give you three guesses when the fun and frolics will start.'

'Tonight?' ventured Thad. 'At the Halloween Carnival?'

'Correcta—' began the Doctor, then stopped. Less

emphatically he said, 'That's right.'

'So what will they do?' asked Martha. 'Cast spells? Hypnotise everyone into that mincing machine of a spaceship?'

'Oh no, it'll be far nastier than that,' the Doctor said. 'They want the terror, remember. The meat's no good without the flavour.'

'So what will they do?' asked Rick. 'Launch an attack?'

'I'd like to see 'em try,' said Scott. 'If we can get everyone ready—'

'Shush,' said the Doctor rudely. 'It won't be that either. The Hervoken might be big and scary, but they aren't physically strong. They'll use agents.' He picked up the book and brandished it. 'Just like they'll use agents to try and get this back.'

'What kinds of agents?' asked Martha.

'Like the leaves,' said the Doctor. 'Like the cats.'

'Something wicked this way comes?'

He nodded grimly. 'Exactly.'

TEN

Twenty minutes later the five of them were sitting in Harry Ho's. The boys were shovelling ice cream into their faces as if it was the last meal they would ever have. Martha was nursing a cappuccino and staring at the Doctor, who had gone into brooding mode. He had ordered a banana split, but it was sitting untouched and melting in front of him. Scott finished his strawberry sundae in half a dozen quick bites and asked in an ice-cream-muffled voice, 'You gonna eat that?' The Doctor gave no indication that he'd heard him, but, as if acting independently, his hand reached out and pushed the bowl across the table.

Loath though she was to break his scowling reverie, Martha finally asked, 'Couldn't we offer them an alternative?'

The Doctor looked up. 'What?'

'The Hervoken. Isn't there something else they could use as fuel?'

'Ever been buried in the sand?' the Doctor asked.

Martha was getting more accustomed to the Doctor's conversational curveballs and took this one in her stride. 'When I was a kid,' she said, 'Leo and Tish once buried me up to my neck on Cromer beach – not that I wanted them to.'

'Imagine being buried in the sand and having a handful of pebbles placed on your stomach. What would happen when you stood up?'

She shrugged. 'The pebbles would fall off.' Then her eyes widened. 'Oh, I get it. The pebbles are Blackwood Falls and I'm—'

'The Hervoken ship,' confirmed the Doctor. 'Even if there *was* a fuel alternative, the ship would incinerate the town when it took off.'

'In that case,' said Martha, 'why don't we destroy that thing?' She nodded at the Necris, which had been placed on the edge of the next table.

'Indestructible,' said the Doctor. 'Or as good as. Chucking it into the middle of an exploding sun might just about do it, but it's infused with so many Hervoken protective doo-dahs that nothing on this planet would even come close to scratching its surface.'

'Why is nothing ever simple?' Martha sighed. Then she sat up straight and slapped her hands decisively on her thighs. 'So come on then, what we gonna do?'

The Doctor tapped his head. 'Think,' he said.

She sat back, lapsing into silence. Then she said, 'Why don't you do what you did last time? Attack them with your blood? Send them loopy?'

'Once bitten, twice shy,' he said. 'They won't fall for that trick a second time.'

'So what *are* we gonna do?' Martha asked, exasperated.

Abruptly the Doctor stood up, his chair screeching backwards. 'There's only one thing *to* do.'

'Which is?'

'I'm going to talk to them.'

Everyone looked at him. 'Cool,' said Thad. 'Can I come too? I want to see what these alien dudes look like.'

The Doctor shook his head. 'This is strictly a solo mission. I need you lot to look after Martha, make sure she goes easy on the cappuccinos. She has a tendency to run around naked when she's got too much caffeine inside her.'

The boys all looked at Martha expectantly. She rolled her eyes. 'He is, of course, joking.'

The Doctor was already striding towards the door.

Martha stood up. 'Hey, you're not going without me.'

The Doctor turned back. His face was deadly serious. 'Yes I am.'

'No way,' she said. 'You need me to watch your back.'

'No, I need you to watch the book.' He pointed at the Necris. 'I'm trusting you to keep that safe while I'm gone. Don't forget, the Hervoken agents will be after it. You'll have to keep on your toes.'

'Anything we can do?' Rick asked.

'Yes, you can go home, lock yourselves in, batten down the hatches. Don't answer the door to funny-looking men, and don't take sweets from strangers.'

He pulled the door open, admitting a few tendrils of green mist.

'Are you sure you'll be OK?' Martha called.

He glanced back once more and grinned at her. 'I'll survive. I always do. See you later.'

Then he stepped out into the mist, closing the door behind him.

It was only lunchtime on his last day of business, but already Jim Tozier was thinking of shutting up shop. He'd done a steady trade in Halloween costumes this morning, but not a roaring one. The weird green mist, which was still hanging about the town, seemed to be discouraging people from venturing out of their houses. The reason Jim *didn't* shut up shop was because some folks still hadn't collected the costumes they'd ordered for tonight's Carnival, and would no doubt be in this afternoon to claim them. He guessed he could always put a note on the door, informing them to call him on his cell phone, but somehow he knew he wouldn't do that. Somehow he knew that, out of a sense of duty and also a sense of *closure*, he'd stick it out to the end.

The real reason he wanted to close up was nothing to do with business, however. Maybe it was simply because he was so tired after a broken night's sleep of weird dreams and disturbing thoughts, but whenever he was alone in the shop Jim couldn't help but feel uneasy. He kept thinking he could see things out of the corner of his eye – costumes stirring, masks turning to face him. He knew it was crazy, but however many times he told himself that, it didn't help. Try as he might, he couldn't shake the feeling that he was being watched.

He sat at the counter, stolidly munching his way through his lunchtime sandwich – ham and salad on rye, with plenty of mustard – and wishing someone else would call by. If they did he would offer them coffee, encourage them to stay a while and shoot the breeze. Part of his edginess, he told himself, could be attributed to the isolating effect of the mist. It crowded against his window like mould, obliterating his view of the usually busy square and plunging the town into perpetual twilight.

Popping his last piece of sandwich into his mouth, Jim was just reaching for the cafetière to pour himself a third coffee – after his night of disturbed sleep he needed the caffeine buzz – when he noticed an odd glow coming from the front of the shop. He paused, his hand hovering in mid-air. What was that? A firefly? Someone shining a torch onto the window from outside?

He licked his lips, once again feeling uneasy, though without knowing why. The glow was green, and hard to pin down. It seemed to drift, to flicker. Jim placed his hands on the counter, needing the reassuring solidity of it. Suddenly his sandwich felt heavy as a brick in his stomach. Almost unwillingly he circled the counter and walked towards the front of the shop.

His feet clumped ominously on the wooden floor. The costumes whispered and stirred in what Jim told himself firmly was nothing but the passing breeze from his body. Cautiously he approached the Halloween window display, an arrangement of pumpkins and masks sprayed with fake cobwebs, in the centre of which stood Sam the Mannequin sporting the Evil Clown costume.

Even when he was close enough to confirm where the glow was coming from, Jim tried to tell himself that what he was seeing couldn't be real. A strange green light was skittering and flickering over the Evil Clown like electricity. Jim told himself it must be an atmospheric thing, some weird but natural phenomenon, like St Elmo's Fire. Maybe a storm was on the way.

Then the hideous rubber clown mask, its empty eye sockets glowing bright green, twisted in his direction.

Jim tried to scream, but his throat was locked. Though the clown's expression was fixed – wide, grinning mouth full of jagged teeth, bulbous green nose, a mass of spiky orange hair – it nonetheless seemed to leer at him. Jim began to back away as the green light in the empty eye sockets intensified. Then, without warning, the light *leaped* out at him, like thick, gloopy ropes of ectoplasm. It clamped itself to his face, filled his mouth and eyes. Jim felt a moment of sheer panic and horror, an instant of white-hot pain…

… and then the pain and the panic passed, and all at once he felt calm and serene – and what was more, he felt *purposeful*. Suddenly he knew without a doubt what he needed to do.

Reaching out, he plucked the Evil Clown mask from the head of Sam the Mannequin and pulled it over his face.

'Why don't you come back to mine?' said Rick.

Martha had been umming and ahhing about what to do, where to go. Should she stay put and wait for the Doctor, or head back to her hotel room and lock herself in? She didn't want to put anyone in danger, but at the same time it might be better, from the point of view of protecting the book, if she had people around her. And besides, from a purely human standpoint, she hated the thought of sitting tight on her own, not knowing how long the Doctor would be or even if he would come back at all. She hesitated for maybe five seconds, and then, not sure whether she was doing the right thing, she said, 'Well… OK. Are you sure your parents won't mind?'

'No way,' said Rick. 'They'll be stoked.'

'I doubt that,' said Martha, 'but cheers for the offer. You ready to go now?'

Rick nodded and the boys rose to their feet. Martha picked up the Necris and tucked it under her arm. Thad, small and bespectacled, said determinedly, 'You stick with us, Martha. We'll protect you.'

Martha laughed, but she felt a little scared inside

– scared for them rather than herself.

'Lead the way, Sir Lancelot,' she said.

Jim stepped into the Evil Clown costume and zipped it up. It was a one-piece, like a set of overalls, patterned in multicoloured harlequin diamonds. There were lacy ruffs at the wrists and ankles, and a long Velcro flap at the front studded with pompom-like buttons that covered the central zipper. Completing the ensemble were a pair of enormous black shoes and ridiculously large white gloves with fat, rounded fingers.

The disquiet that Jim had been feeling last night and today had now disappeared completely. Since the green light had sluiced through his mind he had been feeling good – great, in fact; better than he could remember feeling in a long time. He was calm and clear-headed… and yet despite this he wasn't entirely sure *why* he was dressing himself in the Evil Clown costume. He simply felt a compulsion to do so, that was all. It felt normal. It felt *right*.

Fully kitted out, he clomped over to the full-length mirror beside the counter to see how he looked. It was awkward walking in the giant shoes. He had to lift his feet quite high off the ground, bending his knees so they were virtually at right angles with each step. He couldn't imagine wearing this costume for a long time. As well as becoming quickly exhausted with all the exaggerated walking, it would also be only a matter of time before he would start to feel claustrophobic in the hot, rubbery mask.

He couldn't deny he looked good, though. He filled the costume out well. This was one occasion, Jim thought ruefully, when his paunch actually enhanced the sartorial effect.

He admired himself for a few seconds longer, then decided it was time to take the mask off. It was getting hot; already he could feel sweat trickling down his face. To remove the mask, though, he first had to remove the big white gloves. He tucked one of them into his armpit and tried to yank his hand out of it. But for some reason the hand was stuck; it wouldn't budge. He tried the other hand, with the same result.

Ridiculous, he thought, and tried again. But his hands were well and truly stuck. It was as though they had been super-glued into the white gloves. He started to feel a bit panicky. His head was full of the stifling smell of rubber. He was finding it difficult to breathe.

Maybe he could pull the mask off with the big white sausage fingers. It was only loose rubber, after all. But as soon as he raised his hands, he felt the mask sealing itself to his face.

His panic didn't build slowly this time, but leaped into his head, fully formed. Gone was the serenity he had experienced minutes before, the sense that he was doing the right thing. He clawed at the clown face, but it was no use. He could feel it tightening on his skin, suffocating him. Even worse was the sense that somehow, contained within the rubber, was a vast and evil intelligence. Jim felt it forcing its way into his mind, subsuming his thoughts. He struggled against it, fought to regain control, but it overwhelmed him, crushed him. He felt his thoughts changing, a new personality taking over. In the instant before he was swamped completely, he sensed the nature of this new personality and was horrified by it. It was alien, murderous, utterly deranged…

As soon as they set foot on the pavement outside Harry Ho's, the mist closed in around them. Immediately Martha's head began to dart left and right. She even looked up at the sky, wondering where the first attack would come from. She was hugging the Necris to her chest, both arms wrapped around it. The iron band that the Doctor had fashioned with the sonic and secured snugly around the book seemed to be keeping it quiet for now, for which she was grateful. It was creepy the way the

Necris had been contracting and expanding before – like holding a lump of living flesh in her hands. The Doctor had told her that iron was an effective defence against the Hervoken's power, even better than salt. It blocked and deflected their energy or something. Though to be honest, Martha wasn't too bothered *what* it did as long as it worked.

Flanked by the boys, she crossed the square and began walking past the line of shops on her right. There was a dry cleaner's, a drugstore, an electrical store and an old-fashioned barber's shop with no customers (Martha could see the portly figure of the barber in the brightly lit interior, sitting in his own barber's chair, reading a newspaper). Next was a sandwich shop with a 'Closed' sign on the door, and next to that was a fancy dress place called Tozier's Costume Emporium. They were walking past this when Rick stopped so suddenly that Martha almost stumbled into the back of him.

'Oof,' she said. 'What you doing?'

Rick was staring at the window display. Surrounded by pumpkins and plastic skulls and a couple of broomsticks, and framed by a black sheet festooned with rubber masks and plastic spiders and woolly swathes of cobweb, was a six-foot clown. It had big white hands and a multicoloured harlequin costume and a madly grinning face.

'There's something weird about the clown,' he said.

Scott snorted. 'Come on, man, that dude's been there all week.'

'Yeah, I *know* that,' Rick said with a scowl, 'but it's different to how it was before. More real somehow.'

'Aw, you're just—' Scott began.

But then Thad said, 'Nah, Rick's right. Look at its eyes.'

They all craned forward to peer through the mist. Instead of the previously blank eye sockets, the clown had what appeared to be real, gleaming, staring eyes. What was more, the eyes seemed to be glowing with a soft green light. Thad put his hand flat on the window and leaned forward so that his nose was almost touching the glass…

… and that was when the clown opened its grotesquely wide mouth and grinned at him, revealing a set of gleaming silver teeth, pointed like knives.

As Thad reeled back with a shocked cry, the clown raised its huge hands. Before their eyes its fat sausage-like fingers, encased in snowy-white gloves, suddenly extended into long, bear-like claws.

Scott uttered a single girlish scream and ran off in the direction they had come, his bulky frame swallowed by the mist within seconds. A split-second later, Thad spun round and took off too, cutting diagonally across the square, his actions belying his brave words of only minutes before. Rick, however, simply stood there, staring at the clown, apparently too stunned to flee. Shifting the weight of the Necris into the crook of her left arm, Martha reached out and grabbed his hand.

'Run!' she said.

They ran up the street, passing a whole bunch of other stores that Martha didn't even register. Behind them she heard the shattering of glass, and glanced back to see that the clown had simply jumped through the big plate-glass display window. She saw it standing on the pavement, shaking itself like a dog, shedding shards of glass which tinkled onto the ground around it. Then it came loping after them, its big shoes slapping the pavement as it gave chase. Martha heard it giggling maniacally, but there was nothing jolly in the sound. It was purely and simply the gleeful blood-lust of a predator running down its prey.

Across the square they ran, and up several more streets. Soon they were fleeing through the residential area of Blackwood Falls, along tree-lined pavements edged with picket fences, beyond which pretty clapboard houses nestled at the ends of long, well-clipped lawns. The streets were mostly silent and deserted, and the houses themselves swathed in mist, though dotted here and there Martha could see the faint orange glow from the occasional Halloween pumpkin sitting on someone's front porch.

Despite its vast shoes, and the fact that Martha and Rick were running at full speed, the clown seemed to be keeping pace with them easily. Above their own panting breath, they could hear the rapid slap of its relentless pursuit, each of its footsteps like the crack of a whip. They could also hear its hideous, insane chuckling and the occasional splintering crack of wood as the creature slashed at fences and trees with its curved white claws. Martha tried not to think how much damage those claws would do if the clown got close enough to use them on her, tried instead to concentrate on how they might get out of this without having to give up the Necris, how they could possibly turn the tables or give the creature the slip before they arrived at Rick's house.

What would the Doctor do? she thought, and almost immediately the answer came to her: he'd make use of the available resources. He'd keep his eyes peeled, his mind alert and his senses tuned to his surroundings, in the hope of spotting something – anything – that would give him an advantage.

She looked around as she ran, her eyes scanning the pavement, the road, the lawns. This little patch of suburban America, however, was annoyingly featureless. Where were the twig-covered pits when you needed them? The giant nets that dropped from trees? The trip-wires?

Just as this last thought flashed into her mind, Martha glanced to her left and saw a selection of toys that a child (a girl, she guessed) had left carelessly strewn on her front lawn. There was a pink bike with a white seat and handlebar-tassels, a plastic ball brightly emblazoned with images from *The Little Mermaid*, and a red-handled skipping rope.

It was the rope which gave Martha the idea. Judging that the clown was maybe fifteen seconds behind them, she panted, 'Hang on a sec,' then vaulted the low fence and snatched the rope up off the ground. Jumping back over the fence, she tossed one end to Rick. 'Quick,' she said, 'get behind that tree there, and hold on tight to the handle. When I shout "Now", pull as hard as you can. OK?'

Rick looked scared, but he nodded and scampered to conceal himself behind the tree that Martha had indicated. Holding the other end of the rope, she ducked below the low hedge separating the rope-owner's property from the one next door. As the clown lolloped towards their hiding place, still giggling like a loon, Martha tensed, her stomach roiling, her mouth dry. Every instinct screamed at her to jump to her feet and run like hell, but she resisted, and hoped fervently that Rick would be able to do the same.

Martha's muscles bunched as the clown came closer. She could hear the scythe-like swoosh as its claws whistled through the air. She glanced across at Rick, but his face was a blur in the mist. All she could see of his expression was the glint of his wide, scared eyes.

As the clown came parallel with their hiding-place, Martha screamed, 'Now!' and threw herself backwards as if engaged in a tug of war. For a second she was terrified that she'd yanked the rope right out of Rick's hands, but then she felt a corresponding tug on the other end. The rope, which had been lying slack on the ground between them, tautened, rising into the air. Martha gritted her teeth and held on for all she was worth as the clown's giant shoe became tangled in the rope and it pitched forward, like a diver doing a belly-flop into a swimming pool.

The clown landed flat on its great, grinning face, its hands slapping the ground. It might have been her imagination, but Martha was sure she heard a comical *honk* as the creature's bulbous nose connected with the pavement. In one slick movement, she let go of the rope, grabbed the Necris, which she had put down on the ground beside her, and rose to her feet. She leaped onto the pavement, swung the Necris and brought it slamming down on top of the clown's head, just as it was in the process of bracing its clawed hands on the ground to push itself back to its feet.

There was a flash of green fire, which threw Martha backwards. She went clean over the picket fence and landed next to the pink bike on the toy-strewn lawn. For a moment she lay there, dazed, wondering whether she had been struck by lightning. Then she heard a muffled groaning sound and propped herself up on her elbows. The groaning was coming from the clown, which was lying on its back on the ground, holding its head.

From the murky gloom on the other side of the pavement, a dark shape crept forward. It was Rick, a wary expression on his face. He looked down at the clown and then at Martha.

'I think you broke the spell,' he said. 'When you hit him with the book. I think you bust a connection or something.'

'Careful,' Martha said as Rick took a step closer.

'I think it's OK,' Rick said. 'I think he's just a regular guy in a mask now. Look at his hands. They're back to normal. And his face. It's just rubber again. It doesn't look alive any more.'

Martha scrambled to her feet. Still feeling woozy,

she shook her head. She handed the Necris to Rick and said, 'Give him another whack if he makes any sudden moves.' Then she stepped forward, grabbed a handful of the spiky orange hair and tugged upwards.

The clown mask peeled away to reveal a plump, red-faced man with a bushy white moustache. He blinked confusedly up at her.

'Mr Tozier!' cried Rick.

Her heart still thumping with reaction, Martha said, 'Don't tell me, let me guess – you would have gotten away with it if it hadn't been for us meddling kids?'

The plump man seemed to have no idea where he was. 'Huh?' he said. 'Who are you?'

'I'm Martha,' replied Martha, holding out a hand, 'and despite the lump on your head I reckon I've just done you a favour. Welcome back, Mr Tozier.'

The Doctor strolled into the central chamber, his hands in his pockets. 'Hello there,' he said. 'How's it going?'

The Hervoken drifted towards him, surrounded him. Their leader towered over him, hissing softly.

'It's all right,' the Doctor said, 'you don't have to pretend to look surprised to see me. You knew I was coming, and I know that you knew I was coming. I wouldn't have got this far if you lot hadn't wanted me to. Which is an encouraging sign. It indicates that you're willing to talk, or at least that you're naturally curious about me, which is almost as good. Unless you just want to kill me, of course – which isn't so good. Well, not for me anyway. But I'm willing to take that risk. I mean you're an intelligent bunch. You wouldn't just bump someone off for the hell of it. Er… would you?'

He smiled up into the wide, squashy face of the Hervoken leader. The alien made a number of odd gestures and seemingly arbitrary sounds, which – thanks to the clever old TARDIS – the Doctor understood perfectly.

'I told you,' he said, 'I'm here to talk. I *would* request parlay in compliance with the Shadow Proclamation… but I doubt whether that would mean much to you lot.'

The Hervoken leader made another series of gestures and sounds, which the Doctor interpreted as a question: *What do you want to talk about?* He sensed a certain sneery attitude in the way the question was phrased, however, and suspected that a more literal translation would be something like: *What could you possibly have to say that would be even remotely interesting to us?*

The Doctor dropped the bonhomie and adopted a

more business-like approach. 'I've got a proposition for you,' he said, 'a once-in-a-lifetime offer. I'll take you back to your home world in my TARDIS. That way no one gets hurt. That's it. Simple and straightforward. Take it or leave it.'

The Hervoken looked at each other. The Doctor could almost sense the thoughts zipping between them. Then they did something odd. They began to jerk and shiver. Their long-taloned hands performed erratic little dances in the air. They opened their mouths and ground their jagged teeth together, creating cascading bursts of green sparks, which dissolved like smoke on the air.

The Doctor folded his arms and frowned. 'I'm not laughing,' he said.

The Hervoken leader pointed at him. It uttered a series of arcane words, interspersed with grunts and hisses. It twizzled and stabbed at the air with its fingers.

The Doctor's face grew grim. He recognised a refusal when he saw one. 'In that case,' he said, 'I'm sorry, but I'm going to have to stop you. So don't come crying to me later, saying I didn't give you a chance.'

He shoved his hands back into his pockets and turned sharply on his heel. He was halfway across the chamber floor when a thick black tendril lashed out from the wall and twined itself round his ankle. It was instantly joined by another, which curled itself like a boa constrictor around his upper body, pinning his arms to his sides. Within seconds the Doctor had been rendered immobile, half a dozen of the black vines having wrapped themselves around him. He was lifted up and turned around to face the hovering Hervoken.

'Oh, now I'm really peeved,' he said. 'Now you're *definitely* off my Christmas card list.'

ELEVEN

'**R**ick!' exclaimed Amanda Pirelli, surprised. 'What are *you* doing home? I thought you were helping your dad set up the Carnival.'

'Er… we were, Mom, but something came up.'

She frowned. 'What sort of something?'

'It's complicated,' he said. 'I've brought someone home with me. Is that OK?'

Her frown deepened. 'What do you mean, "someone"? What's going on, Rick?'

'Maybe it'd be better if she explained,' Rick said.

'She? What do you… oh.'

Martha had been hovering outside the kitchen door, but she took Rick's fumbled introduction as a cue to make her entrance. As soon as she stepped into the room, she saw the expression on Rick's mom's face change from bewilderment to alarm, and knew instantly what she was thinking.

'Hiya, Mrs Pirelli,' she said. 'My name's Martha Jones. There's nothing to worry about. Rick's just been helping us out, that's all.'

'Us?' said Amanda, looking from Martha to Rick and then back again. 'What the hell is going on?'

'Like I said, Mom, it's complicated,' said Rick miserably.

'Are you in trouble?' she asked.

'You could say that, yeah.'

Her expression hardened. 'Well, maybe you'd better tell me about it.'

'You'd never believe us.'

'Try me.'

Rick looked desperately at Martha. She said, 'I think maybe you'd better sit down first, Mrs Pirelli.'

Amanda glared at her. 'I will *not* sit down! This is *my* house! Now will someone please tell me what's going on, or shall I call the police?'

Martha sighed and held up the Necris. 'It started when Rick and his friends dug this up,' she said.

'Dug it up? What do you mean, dug it up? Dug it up from where?'

'From under the tree, Mom,' said Rick. 'The black tree at the bottom of the garden? Only it's not really a tree, it's—'

'Let's not jump the gun,' said Martha hastily. She

nodded wearily at the dining table in the centre of the kitchen floor. 'Do you mind if I sit down?'

Amanda pursed her lips, and Martha was sure she was about to say, 'I'd rather you leave.' But then she gave a brief nod, and Martha sank gratefully onto a wooden dining chair.

Haltingly, hesitantly, Martha and Rick told Amanda about the book, the tree, the mist, the Hervoken. It was not easy. Although Rick's mother listened to the story mostly in silence, she did so with an increasingly incredulous expression. When they were done, she blurted, 'Do you honestly expect me to believe all of this?'

'But it's *true*, Mom,' said Rick. 'I swear.'

'Nonsense,' snapped Amanda. 'I don't know *why* this… this woman has been filling your head with such garbage, but I don't—'

And then a quiet voice from the doorway said, 'It *is* true, Mom. Every word.'

They all turned. Chris was standing there, hollow-eyed and haunted. He came into the room. 'I've seen one of them,' he said. 'One of the aliens.' He nodded at Martha. 'I talked to your friend, the Doctor, about it.'

'You've seen…' Amanda said faintly. She slumped back against the kitchen counter, as if the strength had gone out of her legs. 'Where was this?'

'Right out there,' said Chris, pointing at the kitchen window. 'Over by the tree.'

Rick looked at his brother with something like awe. 'What did it look like?' he asked.

'Like something out of a nightmare,' said Chris. 'Ten feet tall, thin, with a great big head and fingers as long as your arm.' He shuddered. 'I don't ever want to see one again.'

'Now do you believe us, Mrs Pirelli?' asked Martha.

Rick's mother looked uncertain; her hands were shaking. 'I don't know,' she said. 'I mean… how can I? It's crazy.'

'What do you think's causing this mist?' said Rick.

'And that earth tremor earlier?' said Chris. 'That was the tree. I know it was.'

Martha was nodding. 'It was the Doctor. He did that. Gave it a drop of his blood. It couldn't handle it.'

'*Alien* blood,' said Rick.

'I need to sit down,' said Amanda.

Chris fetched his mother a chair and she plumped into it gratefully. 'So this book?' she ventured.

'It's called the Necris,' said Martha. 'It's vital to them. It's my job to keep it safe.'

'*Our* job,' Rick corrected her.

'Safe from what?' Amanda asked.

'The Hervoken… well, their agents. The Doctor said they'd send agents to retrieve it.'

'And these agents would be…?'

'Anything,' said Rick. 'The Hervoken can make things come alive.'

At that precise moment they heard a fluttering sound from the hallway outside the kitchen, and then something thumped against the door. The first thump was followed by several others in quick succession. Whatever the objects were, they were small but compact and they had a bit of weight to them.

Martha's initial thought was that the door was being pelted with tennis balls — or at least something of a similar size and shape. She looked at Rick. Having barely recovered from their pursuit by the clown, he was now wide-eyed and pale all over again.

Amanda rose slowly to her feet. 'What *is* that?' she asked fearfully.

'Trouble,' said Martha. 'How strong is that door?'

'Pretty strong,' said Chris.

The rapid thumping abruptly ceased. There was a brief flurry of fluttering movement, like the sound of a bird trapped in a chimney. Moments later this was followed by the tinkle of breaking glass, and then silence.

Martha and the Pirellis crouched – tense, motionless, listening – for maybe half a minute.

'Have they gone?' Rick whispered at last.

'Maybe,' Martha replied, thinking of the breaking glass, though she couldn't honestly believe that whatever had been on the other side of the door would have given up so easily.

She was right. The words were barely out of her mouth when the kitchen window shattered. Amanda screamed and jumped up as broken glass fell into the sink and something black and fluttering entered the room. The black thing flew straight at Martha. She had a split second to register that it was a bat, sporting a gaping mouth of needle-sharp teeth, and then she was swinging the Necris. More by luck than judgement she hit the bat full on. There was a green flash, enough to send a numbing jolt, like an electric shock, down both of her arms, and the bat flopped lifelessly to the ground.

They all stared incredulously at it for a moment, and then in a high, chalky voice, Amanda said, 'It's made of rubber.' She began to laugh hysterically, and then abruptly stopped.

'Is it yours?' Martha asked Rick, clenching and unclenching her hands to try and get the feeling back into them.

Rick nodded. 'I decorated the TV room with them,

'cos that's where me and the guys were planning on hanging out later. I had a big bag of them. They were fifty for five dollars at the Easy Mart…'

His voice tailed off as he realised what he was saying and a look of horror crossed his face.

Martha ran to the broken window and looked out. '*Oh my…*' she whispered.

Swirling ten metres up in the air, like flecks of ash against the green mist, were the rest of the bats. Having abandoned their attack on the stout kitchen door, they had evidently exited the house to search for a more vulnerable point of entry. To Martha they resembled a small but deadly tornado, spinning in a fluttering, silent circle. Even as she watched, however, they re-formed. They stopped their spinning and gathered together in a dense, black mass. Then they began to stream downwards like an unspooling ribbon, heading straight for the house.

'*They're coming!*' she yelled, twisting away from the window. '*Run!*'

Martha stopped just long enough to grab a frying pan off the stove, which she handed to Chris. They all pelted towards the kitchen door. Rick had his hand on the handle and was pulling the door open when the rest of the kitchen windows exploded inwards.

A second later, bats were swooping and diving towards them.

As Chris swatted them with the frying pan and Martha fended them off with the Necris, Rick yanked open the kitchen door and all but shoved his mother ahead of him through the gap.

Martha felt the needle-teeth of the bats scratching her hands, and threw up her arms to stop them plunging their fangs into her face. Chris grabbed the collar of her leather jacket and yanked her backwards through the door. Martha had the presence of mind to grab the handle with her free hand and pull the door shut behind her. One bat, caught half in and half out of the closing door, was crushed into a mangled lump of rubber and fell to the floor, bloodless and inert.

Around a dozen bats had made it out of the kitchen with them. Martha and Chris did their best to fight them off as they ran towards the stairs. Martha had no real idea where they were going. Outside was a no-no; they would be sitting targets in the open. Their best bet was to find a small space that couldn't be breached and lock themselves in. Preferably somewhere without windows – a wardrobe or cupboard, say.

They ran up the stairs and along the upper landing. Chris leaped and whacked a bat with the frying pan as it swooped towards Martha's face. He reminded her of a tennis player, performing a winning smash.

Then he was grabbing her jacket once again, pulling her into the bathroom. When they were inside, Rick slammed the bolt into place. The few bats still pursuing them thumped ineffectually against the door for the next fifteen seconds or so, then stopped.

Once again there was silence. With shaky hands Chris put the frying pan carefully on the floor and wiped sweat from his forehead.

Amanda pointed at Martha with a trembling finger. '*You* brought this on us,' she said.

'*Mom*,' said Rick, appalled, but Amanda silenced him with a glare.

'You've endangered my family,' she said to Martha, her voice full of quiet rage. 'Why did you have to come here?'

Martha looked shamefaced. 'I'm sorry,' she said. 'You're right, and I'm sorry.'

'It's not your fault,' said Rick vehemently. 'Mom, I asked Martha to come.'

Martha held up the hand that was not holding the Necris. She looked oddly as though she was swearing an oath on the Bible. 'No, Rick, your mum's right. I shouldn't have put you in danger. I should have handled this on my own.'

'Yeah, well, we're here now,' said Chris, 'so instead of arguing let's decide what we're gonna do.'

'I don't think there's much we *can* do except wait,' said Martha.

'Wait for what?' Amanda wanted to know.

Martha looked at her. In truth she was a bit stumped. What indeed? However, she said firmly, 'The Doctor.'

'Your friend?' said Amanda, unconvinced and still somewhat hostile. 'So he has all the answers, does he?'

'Usually,' said Martha. 'Or if not, then he makes them up as he goes along. He's pretty good at that.'

'And what if he doesn't come back?' Amanda said.

'He will,' said Martha.

'But what if he doesn't?'

'Then we'll just have to manage, won't we!' Martha said, more sharply than she intended.

'Shh,' said Chris. His ear was pressed to the door. 'I think I hear something.'

They all fell silent and listened. Faintly, but getting louder, they could hear an odd sound. It was a rhythmic series of dry, rattling clicks, like small pieces of wood or stone being rapped together.

'What is it?' whispered Rick.

Martha licked her lips. She was thinking of a scene from a movie she'd watched as a kid, where living skeletons had grown from the scattered teeth of a dead monster.

'I might be wrong – I *hope* I'm wrong – but it sounds to me like bones,' she said.

The rattle-click of movement came up the stairs, along the landing and stopped outside the door. In some ways the few seconds of silence that followed its arrival were even worse than the approaching sounds had been. Chris stepped back from the door, staring at it warily. Martha and Rick exchanged a glance. Amanda retreated to the back of the room, pressing her hands to her mouth as if to stifle a rising scream.

Then there was a crash, and a hairline crack appeared in one of the door's upper wooden panels. Martha looked around desperately for something to defend herself with, but the best weapon available was the one she was already holding. She raised the Necris above her head, readying herself for action. Another crash, and the crack widened, slivers of wood falling inward.

There wasn't much the four of them could do except watch the thing smash its way through the door. With each blow more of the panel splintered and collapsed. Finally a sizeable chunk of wood fell onto the bathroom floor. Immediately a hand and part of an arm thrust its way through the jagged hole it had created.

Just as Martha had feared, the hand was white, fleshless, skeletal. She shuddered at the brittle scraping the twig-like fingers made as they scuttled across the wood towards the bolt. Swallowing her revulsion, she stepped forward and brought the Necris down as if to squash a bug, hoping to disconnect the hand from its spindly wrist, perhaps even to pulverise it. The creature, however, seemed to anticipate her attack and snatched its hand back through the hole just in time.

The momentum of Martha's swing made her stumble forward and drop onto one knee, her face within reach of the hole in the door. The living skeleton on the other side suddenly bent and lunged forward, filling the gap with its chalk-white face, its empty eye-sockets level with Martha's eyes. The skull's lipless jaw creaked wide open, and – though it had no vocal cords – the creature *hissed* at her. Its breath (*How could it have breath? It had no lungs!*) smelled of grave-mould and the dank, sulphurous odour of the Hervoken's lair. Martha recoiled, sprawling on her back on the bathroom floor, coughing and spluttering.

Even as she was pushing herself back up to a sitting position, the creature was reaching through the hole in the door once again. '*Stop it!*' she yelled, but it was too late. The bony fingers wrapped themselves around the bolt and tugged it from its socket. A second later the door swung open and there stood the skeleton, bones clicking and creaking as it shifted its weight. Horribly, impossibly alive.

The Necris was lying on the floor, a few inches from Martha's hand. With frightening speed, the skeleton rushed forward, reached down and grabbed it.

'No!' Martha shouted and made a snatch for it herself, but her fingers closed on empty air. As the skeleton straightened up with its prize, Martha was half-aware of Chris stepping over her, his hands outstretched. She looked up, and saw that he was holding a toilet roll in one hand, a cigarette lighter in the other. She saw him light the toilet roll and then thrust it between two of the skeleton's ribs, jamming it in place. The vertebrae in the skeleton's neck clicked as it tilted its skull to regard the burning wad of paper.

Then, to Martha's astonishment, the creature burst into flames.

It burned surprisingly quickly, fire racing along its network of bones, engulfing it within seconds. It opened its mouth in a soundless scream as it shrivelled and blackened, collapsing in on itself. Its spine snapped and its burning skull tumbled between its charred collar bones and into the crumbling ribcage. The Necris dropped from its lifeless hands and into Martha's arms. Rick and Chris ran forward with wet towels and doused the flames before they could spread and set fire to the house. They smothered the heap of bones and trampled them into burning ash. Seconds later all that was left of the skeleton was black mush and a hazy pall of greenish smoke.

Chris turned to face Martha as she rose to her feet. He had a smudge of soot on his nose and was looking pleased with himself. 'I remembered the bats,' he said.

'Er… good,' replied Martha, who didn't have a clue what he was talking about.

'I remembered they were made of rubber, even when they were alive,' he said, 'and it suddenly made me realise what the skeleton was made of.'

'Ah,' she said. *Now* she understood. She looked at the wet towels and the black gunk dribbling out from underneath. 'Paper?' she said.

'Yeah… well, cardboard. Though I'm not sure how something made of cardboard can smash its way through a door.'

'Hervoken magic,' Martha said, then thought of how the Doctor would frown if he heard her say that. 'Science, I mean.'

'What *I* want to know, Christopher,' Amanda said,

stepping forward, 'is why you had a cigarette lighter in your pocket?'

Suddenly Chris looked like a little boy who'd been caught raiding the cookie jar in the dead of night. 'Er...' he said.

Etta was getting worried. The Doctor should have returned by now.

'If I'm not back by three,' he had told her earlier, 'it means... or it *probably* means... though then again, it *could* just be that...'

'In plain English, if you please, Doctor,' she had said imperiously.

'Well, it will *almost certainly* mean that the Hervoken are not... what's the phrase? Open to negotiation.'

'And what should I do then?' she asked. 'Call the police?'

'Nah, they'd be about as much use as a sherbet umbrella. Your best bet would be to pack up and get out of town as quickly as you can. No, no, hang on... first cancel the Halloween Carnival, initiate some sort of evacuation procedure, and *then* pack up and get out of town as quickly as you can. See ya.'

Three o'clock, he had said. She looked at the big metal clock on her kitchen wall, which had been chopping off the seconds of her life for the past twenty-five years. It read five past three, though, even as she glanced at it, it clunked on another minute. How long should she wait? Perhaps the 'negotiations', as he had called them, were more involved than he had anticipated?

'Come on, Doctor,' she muttered, desperate to hear the sound of his footfalls on the basement steps, willing him to appear like a manic jack-in-the-box in her kitchen. She had no doubt he was the spaceman he had claimed himself to be. He was simultaneously the most unsettling and reassuring man she had ever met, a mesmerising combination of boyish charm and ancient wisdom.

Ten minutes later she stood up. 'Right then,' she said. She had come to a decision. It was the only possible decision she *could* come to. Etta didn't think she was a particularly brave soul, but neither was she the kind of person who would leave a friend in the lurch. She wouldn't flee, as the Doctor had advised, and there wasn't time to fetch help. Which meant there was only one course of action open to her – she would launch a rescue mission. She would get the Doctor back, or die in the attempt.

Arming herself with a torch, she descended the basement steps and lowered herself gingerly into the storage space beneath the floor. The metal door in the side wall was still ajar. She tugged it open and shone her torch into a cramped black tunnel.

Rotting timbers, irregularly spaced, looked to be the only things preventing the tunnel from collapsing in on itself. Etta shuddered, took a deep breath and thought briefly of how this would play havoc with her arthritis. Then she got down on her hands and knees and crawled inside.

'Ow,' said the Doctor. Every time he moved, even just a little bit, the vines securing him flashed green and gave him a zap of energy. It was like being continually jabbed with a cattle prod. 'Can't you turn the juice down on this thing?' he called. 'It tickles.'

The Hervoken ignored him. They had been ignoring him for the past twenty minutes. They were drifting about their central chamber, describing symbols in the air, occasionally chanting or muttering in their breathy, childlike voices. Their movements seemed arbitrary, but the Doctor knew they were conjuring something, that their actions were far more purposeful than they appeared. He hoped Martha was safe. He'd had no choice but to entrust her with the Necris, but he still knew that if anything happened to her because of it, he'd never forgive himself.

He had tried various methods to get the Hervoken to listen to him, but they were having none of it. Perhaps now was the time to take a gamble, therefore, to mix a few home truths in with a dose of good old-fashioned bluffing.

'All right,' he said, 'cards on the table. Your lot don't exist any more. Your people were banished to the deep darkness by the Eternals when your endless, stupid war with the Carrionites threatened to bring this universe and countless others crashing about your... well, I would say ears if you had any.

'Point is you didn't know when to stop, did you? And so the Eternals kicked you out. The only reason they didn't find your little group was because you were already under the earth, dormant. You've been there for thousands of years, that tiny speck of consciousness that kept you alive waiting and waiting for humankind to get clever enough to kick-start your resurrection. You've become legends on this planet, part of folklore. You've seeped into the nightmares of a thousand generations of children.'

He took a deep breath: here came the bluffing part.

'But the irony is, if you get this creaky old ship of yours working again, it'll be like a beacon to the Eternals. They'll find you and they'll stamp you out. You're nothing but a stray bit of dirt to them. A lone germ. A last surviving cockroach. Is that what you really want? A final glorious ascent into the heavens, and then – splat! Bye bye, Hervoken. 'Cos that's what'll happen unless you listen to me.

'I can take you somewhere in my TARDIS where the Eternals'll leave you alone, where they'll let you live out your lives in peace. So come on, boys, whaddya say? Do this thing my way and everyone's a winner.'

Still they ignored him. And then they ignored him some more. The Doctor sighed, scowled. 'All right,' he muttered, 'please yourselves.'

Even while he had been talking, his mind had been working constantly, furiously, trying to think of a way out. He knew there had to be one. There always was. It was just a case of working it out before it was too late.

Something to his left caught his eye: a glimmer of light, different to the swamp-like iridescence that pulsed and flickered and bubbled in the Hervoken's lair. As surreptitiously as he could, the Doctor glanced in that direction. He didn't know whether to feel heartened or dismayed to see Etta appear in the cavernous entrance to the central chamber. He was about to mouth at her to turn off her torch when she noticed the Hervoken for the first time and dropped the torch out of sheer fright. It landed on the ground and broke. A black vine immediately snaked from the wall and snatched it up. Green sparks flew as the vine tightened on the torch, crunching it into mangled pieces of plastic and metal. A nearby Hervoken, apparently alerted by the sound, drifted across. Etta could only stand there, transfixed with shock, as the alien loomed over her.

The Doctor clenched his teeth, waiting for the inevitable. But then, to his astonishment, the Hervoken drifted away, as if the old lady wasn't worth its attention. Why had it simply ignored her? Was it something to do with her age? Her lack of physical threat? And then it came to him.

'Pssst,' he said. Etta hadn't spotted him yet. She was too overawed by the crawling walls and the Hervoken themselves.

She turned her head and blinked in his direction. Back-lit by pulsing green light, the walls writhing around her, she looked endearingly out of place. She dithered a moment, glanced at the Hervoken again. The Doctor flicked his head in a 'c'mere' gesture, and received another painful zap for his troubles.

Her eyes and mouth wide in terrified awe, moving almost as if she was shell-shocked, Etta plodded across to him. The Hervoken paid her no attention whatsoever. The Doctor almost laughed out loud.

'As you can see, I got a bit tied up,' he whispered.

Etta stared at him. 'Are those things really aliens? I feel as if I'm dreaming.'

'Yep, they're aliens,' said the Doctor casually. 'And

so am I. And so are you, come to that. We're all aliens together.'

'Why are they ignoring me?' she asked.

The Doctor grinned. 'They don't see you as human,' he said. 'You and your ancestors have absorbed so much Hervoken energy over the past couple of hundred years that they see you as part of themselves, part of their ship. I reckon when they turned the cats on us yesterday, you could have just stood there and they'd have run straight past you.'

'Now he tells me,' said Etta drily, making the Doctor grin again. 'So what do I do to get you out of here?'

'Well, if I'm right,' said the Doctor, 'you should be able to make these things release me just by thinking about it. Put your hands on the vines, close your eyes and command them to let go with your mind. *Believe* you can do it. Think like a Hervoken.'

'All right, I'll give it a try,' said Etta dubiously. After a moment's hesitation she placed her hands on a couple of the vines entwined around the Doctor and squeezed her eyes closed. For a minute or more she stood motionless, holding her breath, and then she blurted, 'Nothing's happening.'

'Try harder,' urged the Doctor. '*Imagine* the vines loosening, going limp and floppy. *You're* the boss, Etta, not them. *You're* the one in control. Just be your natural stroppy self and you'll be laughing.'

'Hmph,' she said, but she squeezed her eyes closed again and scrunched up her face, redoubling her efforts. The Doctor cheered her on silently, and after a few seconds he felt the vines beginning to loosen. He pulled one arm free, then the other. Seconds later the vines simply sagged from him, slumping to the floor and crawling sluggishly back to the wall, like injured snakes.

'Oh, top job, Mrs Helligan,' he whispered. 'Now let's scarper before they notice.'

They began to hurry across the central chamber towards the door. They were halfway across when they heard what in Hervoken-speak amounted to cries of alarm – a mass of agitated, sibilant whispers.

'Keep going,' the Doctor muttered to Etta, and turned round. The Hervoken were flowing towards him, taloned hands outstretched. More vines were detaching themselves from the walls, snaking in his direction.

The Doctor whipped his sonic from his pocket, turned it on and held the business end to his wrist.

'Stop!' he shouted, and amazingly everything did. The Hervoken hovered in the air, facing him; the vines twitched and curled, but stayed where they were.

'Either let me go or I'll open this vein here and now,' he said. 'You might have worked out how to cope with a *few* drops of the hard stuff, but a whole armful of top-grade diesel in a lead-free engine? Very nasty. And don't think for a second that I *won't* sacrifice myself to cripple this ship and save the people up there. Because I've already got far too many deaths on my conscience and I'll do whatever it takes not to get any more.'

He glared at the Hervoken, relaying through his thought waves and his body language that he meant every word. From the corner of his eye, he saw Etta hurrying away. The Hervoken regarded him for several long seconds, drifting in the dank subterranean air, like flotsam on the tide. Then their leader made a dismissive gesture: *Go.*

The Doctor nodded slowly and backed away, sonic still pressed to his wrist.

'Wise decision,' he said.

TWELVE

Martha hesitated, then tapped on the door. 'Doctor?'

There was no answer, so she tried again, and this time was rewarded with a distracted, 'Hmm?'

'Can I come in?' she asked.

'Mm,' he said.

She took that as a yes, so she opened the door.

The Doctor was sitting cross-legged on Chris's bed, staring broodily down at the Necris. He had arrived at the Pirellis' an hour before, having made an educated guess that Martha would be there after trying the hotel first. He had listened to Martha's account of the various attempts the Hervoken had made to get their property back, and had made the requisite sounds of distress and sympathy when Amanda Pirelli had gone on about the damage done to her house. But Martha had sensed he was distracted, and as soon as he could he had shut himself away with the Necris, saying that he needed some time to study it, to discover some chink in the Hervoken's armour.

'It's starting to get dark,' she said now.

'Is it?' He swung his head up as though roused from a trance, and peered at the deepening mist outside the window. 'Oh yeah…'

'How you getting on?' she asked, perching on the edge of the bed.

He shrugged and grunted. He was evidently not in a communicative mood.

Martha tapped the iron band encircling the Necris. 'It's been quiet for a while now. No more attacks. Maybe the Hervoken have decided we're too much of a match for them.'

'Doubt it,' murmured the Doctor. 'They're more likely conserving their energy for the big showdown.'

'Is that what *you're* doing?' asked Martha, and was rewarded with the hint of a smile.

Instead of answering, however, the Doctor asked, 'What time is it?'

'I thought *you* were supposed to be the expert,' she teased, then said, 'About five.'

'Couple of hours to the Carnival,' he said.

'Isn't there *any* way we can stop it? Warn the townspeople? Call a meeting?'

'They'll all be too busy apple-bobbing and stuffing themselves full of pumpkin pie by now,' he said. 'Besides, do you honestly think they'd believe us? They'd run us out of town.'

Martha sighed. 'Haven't you got *any* sort of plan?'

'Oh, I'll just do what I always do,' said the Doctor.

'Which is?'

He raised his hands like a boxer, feinted to the left. Suddenly she sensed the energy flowing back into him.

'Roll with the punches,' he said.

Rick unhooked his werewolf costume from the back of his door and held it up. He looked at it for a long time, then sighed. He remembered how excited he'd been when he'd collected it from Tozier's yesterday. It seemed like a lifetime ago now.

He couldn't believe how his entire perception of life had changed in the past twenty-four hours. After school yesterday he'd been looking forward to nothing more than trick-or-treating, going to the Carnival, and watching a bunch of horror movies with his friends. Now all of that seemed like kids' stuff, trivial and pointless. He threw the costume onto the bed. He wouldn't be wearing it this year.

He'd always thought monsters were cool, but not any more.

Where would he be this time tomorrow, he wondered. Would he still be alive? Would Blackwood Falls still be standing? He looked out of his window. The green mist was the colour of sludge now, slowly deepening to black. Rick stared at it, and wondered whether he'd ever see daylight again.

The lights from the Carnival showground shone faintly through the thick green mist. The pop music blaring from the loud speakers sounded tinny and distorted. On another day the smell of hot dogs, burgers and candyfloss (or cotton candy, as they called it here) would have set Martha's stomach rumbling, but tonight she was too nervous to be hungry, too wired to focus on anything but the potential showdown ahead.

She glanced at the Doctor. Her tension made the picture on the rucksack he was wearing seem funnier than it actually was. She giggled at the image of Jar Jar Binks grinning inanely back at her.

'You look such an idiot wearing that,' she said.

He ran his hands over the front of his suit as though smoothing out the creases, an indignant look on his face. Then he realised what she was actually referring to.

'Oh, *this*,' he said, and jiggled his shoulders so that the rucksack – and the picture of Jar Jar – bobbed up and down. 'Hey, don't knock the Binks clan. They're good people. Very hospitable.'

'Yeah, right,' she laughed.

'No, I'm serious. Old George thought Jar Jar was a figment of his imagination, but people often mistake telepathic messages for their own ideas.'

Now Martha looked uncertain – and a little horrified. 'You *are* joking, right?'

The Doctor raised his eyebrows and waggled them mischievously. 'Mind you, he was *way* off the mark with all that stuff in Episode 9.'

Martha turned at the sound of running footsteps. Was this it, she wondered, the first attack?

Two figures appeared out of the mist. The Doctor stepped towards them angrily.

'I thought I told you to stay at home.'

Chris bridled. 'You're not my dad.'

'This is going to be dangerous,' Martha said reasonably.

'We know. But we can't just sit at home doing nothing,' said Chris. 'This is our town, not yours.'

'It's not even your planet,' Rick pointed out, trying not to quail as the Doctor glared at him.

There was silence for perhaps five seconds, then the Doctor gave an exasperated sigh and spun on his heel. 'Humans,' he muttered. 'It's your funeral, I suppose.' He stalked away.

'Stick close to us and don't do anything stupid,' said Martha.

'Whatever,' muttered Chris.

They passed through the entrance arch and into the showground, paying their entry fee as they went. To Martha the brash cheerfulness of the overhead music seemed enforced, masking an underlying tension. Maybe it was her imagination, but many of the townsfolk seemed wary, apprehensive. The adults especially – murmuring to friends and neighbours in low voices, drifting aimlessly from stall to stall – looked as if they were only going through the motions of enjoying themselves. She wondered whether they had some premonitory sense of what to expect, having lived unwittingly on top of the Hervoken ship for so many years. Or maybe it was simpler than that. Maybe it was merely the effect of the green mist, working on the fear centres of their brains.

The kids, at least, seemed relatively unaffected by the tension evident in their elders. Children from three upwards were running around, shrieking and laughing, dragging their parents from pillar to post, resplendent in their many and varied Halloween costumes. Wherever Martha looked, she saw miniature witches and demons, zombies and vampires, skeletons and ghosts.

She, the Doctor and the boys strode through the crowds of excited children and subdued adults, suspicious and alert. The Doctor sniffed the air at regular intervals.

'So far so good?' said Martha.

'Hm,' he said noncommittally.

They wandered over to a stall where the object was to throw darts into playing cards stuck to a board. *ACES WIN PRIZES!* announced the sign overhead.

'Try your luck, buddy?' said a portly man in a chequered coat and bow tie.

Distractedly the Doctor picked up a dart and threw it without really looking. It flew straight as an arrow and hit the Ace of Spades dead centre.

'Whoa,' exclaimed Rick and Chris in unison.

'Well, I'll be…' said the portly man.

'Show-off,' murmured Martha, trying not to look impressed.

'You won the top prize, buddy. Take your pick,' said the man.

The Doctor was still peering around the showground. 'You choose, Martha,' he said vaguely.

Martha pointed. 'I'll have the cuddly orang-utan, thanks.'

It was almost life-size, with long arms and hands

fastened together with Velcro. The stall owner looped it around Martha's neck.

'What am I supposed to do with this?' she asked as they walked away.

'Do you want a serious answer to that question?' replied the Doctor.

Martha offered it to the boys. Chris gave her a withering look and shook his head. Rick looked momentarily tempted, then shook his head too.

They did another circuit of the showground. Martha gave the orang-utan to a little girl dressed as a spider, who was getting off the carousel. The girl's mother looked suspicious until Martha said, 'I'm going back to England soon and can't fit it in my luggage.'

As they passed the hot dog stand for the second time, Martha's stomach turning over at the smell of frying onions, a sheepish voice from behind them said, 'Hi.'

Turning, they saw Thad in his mummy/ghoul costume, his body wrapped in bandages, his face deathly white aside from his lips and the hollows around his eyes, which were black. He was wearing the expression of a disobedient dog expecting a kick from its owner.

'You got away then?' he said.

'Yeah,' Rick said heavily, 'no thanks to you.'

Thad squirmed. 'I'm really sorry, Rick. I panicked.
I was gonna call you, but I was scared in case…' he
tailed off.

Rick said nothing, simply stuck his hands in his
pockets and scowled.

'It's all right, Thad,' Martha said. 'It was a natural
reaction under the circumstances. I mean, we *all* ran
– *didn't we, Rick?*' She looked at him pointedly.

Rick shrugged. 'I guess.'

'So we're OK then?' said Thad.

Rick looked at him a moment longer, then the
scowl left his face, the tautness went out of his
body.

'Yeah, sure, man.'

They shook hands.

All at once the Doctor stiffened, drawing himself
to his full height. Although Martha had been
expecting trouble, she still shuddered at the grim
intensity of his expression.

'Something wicked…?' she asked.

'…this way comes,' he confirmed in a murmur.
He bared his teeth at her like an ape.

'Itching again?'

'Oh yes,' he said.

The eerie chanting of the Hervoken rose to a
crescendo. Their fingers twitched and flickered as

they scratched fiery green sigils in the air. The black vines thrashed like trees in a frenzied storm, rippling with thick, soupy clots of glaucous light.

The aliens were gathered in a circle, at the centre of which a crackling vortex was beginning to form. The vortex resembled a spinning tunnel composed of green smoke, a vaporous whirlpool lying on its side, which stretched ten, twelve metres into the air. As though obeying a silent command, one of the Hervoken drifted forward, clothes flapping in black tatters around it, and entered the vortex. The instant it had disappeared, a second Hervoken moved forward, and then a third.

Oddly, however, even though the number of aliens left in the chamber was dwindling, their chanting was not. It echoed around the chamber as though the very walls were imbued with it, as though their incantation, ancient and powerful and deadly, had taken on a terrible life of its own…

A wind sprang up around the showground, making the plastic awnings of the various stalls flap and billow, the loops of coloured lights rattle like bones.

The Doctor, teeth clenched, hair blowing, ranged from side to side, peering up into the misty sky.

Suddenly he pointed. 'Here it comes!' he yelled.

Martha followed the direction of his finger.

Something was happening to the mist. Slowly it was beginning to spin, like water running down a plughole. The eye of the vortex was maybe thirty metres above them, but at its centre, instead of darkness, she could see a pulsing, rhythmic glow. It was faint at first, but as she watched it grew steadily brighter and began to expand outwards. It was as though something was coming, some celestial visitation, approaching through a tunnel of light.

Everyone had seen it now. Everyone had stopped what they were doing to stare up, awestruck and fearful. The only movement came from the fairground rides on the far side of the field. The only sound was the music still blasting from the loudspeakers, an inane accompaniment to a spectacle as breathtaking as it was ominous.

The glow increased until it was a ball of blazing light, a miniature sun, which illuminated the night sky and cast a sickly pallor across the proceedings below. The townsfolk began to murmur in fear, to gather their children close.

All at once, multiple tendrils of green light erupted from the centre of the vortex like an exploding firework. Each of the tendrils sought out a different child, encircling their victims in crackling loops of luminescence.

As the green fire skittered up and down their

bodies, the children stood rigid, their faces (those that weren't concealed behind masks) expressionless, their eyes staring ahead. Some parents screamed or began to cry. Martha heard a mother shouting 'Jeb!' over and over again. She heard another woman screech, 'No! Leave my girl alone!' She even heard one father say angrily, 'Come on, Jason, quit fooling around,' as if this was some mass practical joke concocted by the children themselves.

The kids, however, seemed oblivious to the anguish of their parents. Martha looked around, helpless and horrified, wishing there was something she could do. She half-turned to speak to the Doctor, but then felt a hand tugging at the sleeve of her leather jacket, an anxious voice calling her name. Turning in the opposite direction, she looked into Rick's wide-eyed face.

'Look at Thad,' he said.

Like most of the other kids, Thad was encased in a funnel of shimmering light. Also like the others, he was standing immobile, his expression slack, mouth hanging open. But as Martha looked at him, she realised something else was happening too. Slowly, subtly, Thad was beginning to change. His face was becoming wizened, his skin turning to parchment. The bandages around him were tightening, ageing, acquiring a patina of mould and dust. The very shape of his body was altering – his bones elongating, his hands twisting into claws. His skull was stretching, his brow getting heavier. He was starting to hunch forward like an ape.

'Doc—' Martha began. And then she realised a similar transformation was overcoming all the other children. Kids dressed as werewolves were growing taller, more bestial, their fingers lengthening into talons, real fur springing up on their bodies; those dressed as witches were turning into withered crones, their hideous, bent-nosed faces developing warts and boils; those who had come as vampires were becoming sallow, their incisors lengthening to sharp points.

It was happening all around the showground. Children were actually turning into the creatures they had dressed up as. They had just one common factor: the eyes of each were glowing a vivid, putrescent green.

The changes took maybe fifteen seconds. Then the lassoes of light round the children's bodies withdrew, snapping back into the blazing eye of the vortex, like a vast creature retracting its tentacles. Horrified parents backed away from their kids. The monsters began to snarl and roar and hiss as they straightened up. They stretched their transformed muscles and shook their heads, as though throwing off the effects of a deep sleep. Some raised their claws and looked around, taking a renewed and deadly interest in their surroundings.

'Oh my God,' Martha said, feeling sick, 'they're going to get the kids to kill their parents, aren't they?'

'Their parents and then each other,' said the Doctor grimly. 'They need the terror *and* the blood.'

'That's *horrible*.'

'To the Hervoken, it's just like pulling in at the petrol station and filling up the tank.'

'How do we stop it?' Martha asked.

'Stay alive for a start,' said the Doctor.

Before she could respond, he grabbed the collar of her jacket and yanked her backwards. The transformed Thad's claw-like hand swiped through the space where her head had been a split second before. Martha caught a glimpse of Thad's snarling, green-eyed, utterly inhuman face. Then she and the Doctor were tumbling backwards over the low counter of a home-made jewellery stall, scattering the carefully arranged displays of earrings and brooches and bracelets.

The owner of the stall, a young woman with henna-red hair and a baggy jumper, had already taken refuge beneath the counter, and screamed as the Doctor and Martha sprawled before her. Like a cat, the Doctor sprang upright in an instant.

'Shh,' he said. 'It's OK. You stay there. You'll be fine.'

Crouching low, he peered over the counter and was joined seconds later by Martha. The scene before them was one of sheer pandemonium.

Adults were running, screaming, from their children, who were pursuing them with murderous intent; a huge spider (probably the girl she had given the orang-utan to, Martha realised with a thrill of horror) was scaling the metal framework of the now-motionless Ferris wheel to reach the terrified adults trapped in the upper cars; over by the main marquee, a group of adults were fending off a ravening horde of monsters with tables and chairs; nearby, Rick was lying on the ground with Thad's hands round his throat, whilst Chris had his arms wrapped round Thad's chest and was trying to drag him away.

Martha scrambled over the counter to give Rick and Chris a hand. Thad was drooling and snapping, his teeth long and yellow. If Chris hadn't been holding him, Martha had no doubt he would be trying to rip Rick's throat out. She looked around for something to use and spotted a second-hand bookstall. She crossed to it, grabbed the biggest hardback she could find, then ran back over to the three boys and swung the book at Thad's head. It connected with a hefty *thunk* and Thad's grip loosened on Rick's throat. She was about to deliver another blow when a voice shouted, 'Stop!'

It was the Doctor. 'Don't hurt him,' he said. 'Whatever they look like, remember they're still only children.'

'What are we supposed to do?' gasped Chris, still struggling with the half-dazed Thad. 'Reason with him?'

'Let me,' said the Doctor, dropping to his knees beside Rick's prone body and facing the bandaged ghoul that Thad had become. He reached out with both hands, then quickly snatched one back as Thad twisted and snapped at his fingers like a dog. He blew in Thad's face to distract him, then tried again, both hands snaking in to grip Thad's thrashing head. He pressed his thumbs into Thad's temples, and immediately the ferocious expression slipped from the boy's face. His eyes closed and he slumped forward in Chris's arms.

'Lower him to the ground gently,' said the Doctor, then swiftly examined Rick's throat. 'You OK, Ricky boy?'

Rick swallowed and winced, then nodded groggily. 'Fine,' he croaked.

'Good man.'

Chris was looking at Thad, who was now snoring gently. 'What was *that*?' he marvelled. 'Vulcan death-grip?'

'Lepscillian massage technique,' said the Doctor. 'He'll feel refreshed and bountiful when he wakes up.'

'Bountiful?' queried Martha.

'Lepscillians' favourite word. It's all bountiful this and bountiful that on Lepscillia. Drives you bonkers after a while.'

He stood up and looked around, his jaw clenching as he took in the scene around him. Fifty metres away a group of demons, most of them horned and red-skinned, were laying siege to a burger van. The beleaguered members of staff were throwing whatever they could find at the attacking creatures: cutlery, cooking utensils, frozen burgers, even bread rolls. The demons, lithe and agile as apes, were shaking the van, leaping onto the roof, clawing at the staff through the side opening.

'No,' breathed the Doctor as one of the staff members panicked and made a break for it out of the back doors. He was a skinny guy of around twenty, with curly hair and a scrappy beard. Although fear lent him an impressive turn of speed, he was no match for the trio of demons which broke away from the larger pack to pursue him. They fell on him like a pride of lions upon a gazelle. As the man began to scream, the Doctor looked away, his face furious, and swung his rucksack from his back.

'*Chris!*' shouted Martha as a zombie came shambling up behind him, arms outstretched. Chris threw himself forward, rolling over and springing to his feet. The Doctor tore open the rucksack and lifted out the Necris. With one blast of the sonic the iron band securing it broke into two pieces and fell to the ground. The Doctor held the Necris above his head.

'This stops *now*!' he yelled, pressing the still-active sonic against the Necris's cover. The fleshy material began to ripple and shudder as though in pain. 'Show yourselves, Hervoken, or your precious book gets it.'

There was a bubbling and a boiling from the centre of the vortex, and suddenly there they were, a dozen or more Hervoken, materialising out of thin air. They hovered ten metres above the ground, in a wide circle around the Doctor, tall and spindly, like great black carrion crows.

Rick gasped at his first sight of the aliens and dropped to his knees. Chris moaned and cowered in fear. Martha clenched her fists, but stood her ground, shoulder to shoulder with the Doctor.

Hair still blowing around his head, arms raised

aloft, the Doctor shouted, 'Right, this is the deal. Listen carefully. I'm not open to negotiation. You put an end to this slaughter *now* or I'll destroy the Necris. And don't think I can't or I won't, because I can and I will. I've broken through every one of its defences, and all I have to do is increase the sonic frequency by another few levels, and your indispensable little starter motor will be dust. And don't think you can snatch it away with your spells either. The sonic field has been configured to deflect any rescue attempt. You try to transmat this beauty and your energy will bounce right back atcha. As long as *my* sonic is in contact with *your* Necris, you can't do a thing, you can only listen.'

He paused briefly and looked around the circle of Hervoken, his expression steely. Then he said, 'OK, what's going to happen is this. The people of Blackwood Falls want you out of their town and off their planet. So you put an end to this *now* and I'll find you another source of fuel – one that doesn't involve killing people. I can do it, easy. I'm good with engines. Soon as the ship's ready, we'll clear the town and you can vamoose. All right, you'll wreck a few houses, but so what? Houses are just *things*, aren't they? They're not *important* – like people, like *lives*. This way you get your Necris back *and* you get to keep your ship. Course, you'll have to keep an eye out for the Eternals whilst you're up there, but that's your problem. Once you're off this planet, our association ends.'

Despite the continuing screams and cries and roars, not to mention the still-blaring music, the echoes of the Doctor's voice seemed to ring out around the showground. The Hervoken regarded him impassively, not responding.

'Well, come on,' the Doctor shouted, 'I haven't got all—'

Something swooped from the sky, seeming to appear from nowhere. Martha ducked, thinking it was a huge bird, an eagle perhaps. The flying creature snatched the book from the Doctor's hand before he had a chance to alter the frequency of the sonic. Martha saw that it was some kind of sprite or evil fairy – doubtless another of the transformed children. She looked back at the Doctor, still not entirely sure what had happened, and saw an expression of horror on his face.

'No!' he shouted.

The Hervoken leader gave a triumphant hiss and performed a magician-like flourish whose meaning was patently obvious: *You lose*. The Doctor and Martha could do nothing but watch as the sprite delivered the Necris into the Hervoken leader's hands. The alien opened its mouth wide in what

Martha could only think of as a gloating grin and muttered a quick incantation. A fizzing green light enveloped the Necris, and it faded away...

...to reappear seconds later in the hollow on top of the central dais in the main chamber of the Hervoken ship. Instantly the mass of claw-like roots fringing the hollow clamped into place over the book, like the jaws of a Venus flytrap closing on an unsuspecting insect.

Martha felt numb. They had lost. The Doctor had made the silliest, most fundamental mistake by not looking behind him, and suddenly it was all over.

As some of the hideous creatures that had once been children closed in on them, Martha thought of her family: her mum and dad, and her brother Leo and her sister Tish. She thought of her flat and her job back in London, thought of how her life had changed so irrevocably in such a short time, of all the amazing things she'd done. She'd seen Shakespeare's England and 1930s New York; she'd been on the prison planet Volag-Noc and travelled on real-life spaceships; she'd survived encounters with Plasmavores and Daleks, real-life witches and giant, pollution-guzzling crabs. And now it was all going to end here, ripped apart by a bunch of possessed children. As though he sensed her thoughts, the Doctor took her hand in his and gave it a squeeze.

She looked up at him. His face was sombre, almost wistful. 'You really shouldn't have done that,' he murmured to the Hervoken. Then he held up his sonic screwdriver.

The Necris convulsed, sending a shock wave through the Hervoken ship. Then, like a giant sponge, it began to absorb energy, to suck the already thin life-blood from the veins of the vessel at an incredible speed. Ripples of energy flowed from the thrashing vines. The central dais pulsed and shimmered as the ship's entire stock of reserve power converged on it.

Like a heart engorged with blood, the Necris began to swell and rupture. As it absorbed more power than it was designed to hold, it started to glow fiercely, like a reactor core reaching critical mass. A high-pitched whine filled the Hervoken ship – a whine that escalated rapidly into what sounded like a scream of unbearable pain...

The ring of transformed children closing in on the Doctor, Martha, Rick and Chris suddenly stopped. Some of the creatures stood stock-still, like soldiers awaiting orders, whilst others began to sway and stagger about in confusion.

One child, which had become a hulking Frankenstein's monster with a scarred, patchwork face and clomping lead boots, raised its hands to its head and dropped to its knees with a groan. As Martha watched, she saw the greenish lustre fade from the children's eyes, and then a ripple of energy leave each of their bodies and spiral upwards into the vortex of mist. The image made her think of a mass of souls vacating the bodies of the dead. However, these children were not dying; instead, they were being given *back* their lives.

The instant the energy left them, each of the kids reverted to how they had been before the Hervoken spell had consumed them. As they became themselves again, they looked around, dazed and shocked, as if waking from a collective nightmare. A few burst into tears; some cried out for their parents. Martha watched the Frankenstein's monster peel the mask from its face and realised it was Rick's friend, Scott.

Meanwhile, something was happening to the Hervoken. They were beginning to thrash about like black sheets in a strong wind, to wail in their thin, childlike voices. The Doctor watched them unblinkingly, his face like thunder, sonic still held out before him, its piercing warble splicing the air.

The thrashing of the Hervoken became

increasingly more frenzied. Martha thought of animals caught in traps, struggling desperately to escape. She saw their huge pale heads beginning to blacken and shrivel, their eyes sinking into their sockets, their many-jointed fingers curling up like burning twigs. Finally, their bodies began to crumble away, like vampires in sunlight, and within seconds they were nothing but ribbons of black ash, streaming into the centre of the vortex.

With the Hervoken gone, the green mist, which had shrouded Blackwood Falls since the Necris had been unearthed over twenty-four hours earlier, began rapidly to disperse. It too drained into the vortex, the radiance at the centre of which gradually faded and shrank until there was nothing left but darkness.

Once the mist had cleared, the vortex itself dwindled and died, simply petering out like a spent tornado. Suddenly Martha realised that for the first time since they had arrived she could see stars twinkling in the night sky. She took a deep breath, relishing the cold, clean sharpness of the air.

She turned to the Doctor and was about to speak when she heard and felt a deep, subterranean rumble. Almost immediately the night sky some distance away was illuminated by a harsh white glow, which surged upwards before disintegrating into a million greenish sparks that winked out as they fell slowly back to earth.

'What was that?' asked Rick in a small, shocked voice.

Martha began to shake her head, and then all at once it came to her.

'It was the Hervoken ship, wasn't it, Doctor? The tree. You did something to the book, didn't you? Drained off their energy.'

The Doctor, his face grim, turned off his sonic and pocketed it before giving her a curt nod.

'Never underestimate the power of the printed word,' he said. 'End of story.'

The Doctor and Martha stood with the Pirelli family, staring into the ash-filled crater at the bottom of the garden. There was no trace whatsoever of the black tree. Not a single twig had survived.

'I don't believe this,' Tony Pirelli kept saying, shining his torch down into the hole. 'I just don't believe it.'

The Doctor said nothing.

His face was expressionless, his hands stuffed in his pockets. It was Martha who had insisted on taking the boys home. The Doctor had wanted to slope off without saying goodbye, leaving the Blackwood Falls townsfolk to pick up the pieces of their lives.

'Believe me,' he had said to her, 'it's easier that way.'

'For who?' she had demanded, and he had just sighed.

In the end, he had agreed to stay a bit longer. He might be the one who usually called the shots, but when she dug her heels in, when she made it known that something was important to her, he was usually OK about it.

People had died tonight. Wherever they went, people *always* died. And Martha thought part of the reason the Doctor never wanted to stick around afterwards was so that he didn't have to come to terms with that. Maybe he thought that death followed him around, that when people died it was his fault. He had saved countless lives even in the short time she had been with him, but he never failed to be haunted by the ones he *didn't* save.

Rick looked up at the Doctor now with something like awe. 'What did you do?' he asked.

'I subverted the kinetic flow of the energy generated by the Necris,' the Doctor replied. 'It caused the ship to implode.' He sounded almost ashamed.

'Huh?' said Rick.

'He made their spells run backwards,' said Martha, knowing she was massively oversimplifying what in reality was no doubt a very convoluted and technical explanation. 'He undid everything the Hervoken had done.' Suddenly a thought struck her. 'Hey, does this mean Mr Clayton will have got his mouth back?'

'S'pose,' muttered the Doctor.

'Well, that's *good*, isn't it?' she said, trying to cheer him up.

'Hmm,' he replied.

'So this Necris thing?' said Chris. 'You changed it with your little torch? When you were hanging out in my room this afternoon?'

'It wasn't hard,' said the Doctor almost apologetically. 'It was just a bit of basic tinkering.'

'The hard bit was convincing the Hervoken they'd beaten you,' said Martha. 'You certainly fooled me.'

The Doctor shrugged. 'They'd have been suspicious if I'd just given the Necris back to them, even if I'd made it sound like an exchange for the lives of the townspeople. They'd have checked it over and found out what I'd done. I knew our only chance was to make them think they'd outsmarted me. They were hoist with their own petard.'

'But what if they'd agreed to your terms?' said Martha. 'Would you have fixed the Necris for them and let them destroy the town?'

The Doctor frowned. 'I knew they wouldn't.'

'But what if they *had*?'

He looked at her, and his eyes suddenly seemed as black and depthless as space. 'I gave them their chance,' he said evenly. 'They didn't take it.'

Martha saw Tony and Amanda Pirelli looking at the Doctor almost warily, and knew what they were thinking: *Is this the kind of person we want our boys hanging around with?*

'Excuse me, mister,' Tony said almost hesitantly, 'but who exactly *are* you again?'

'I'm just a traveller, passing through,' the Doctor said.

'What's *that* supposed to mean?' asked Amanda.

The Doctor shot Martha a look: *See? I told you it was easier to just leave.*

A voice came floating out of the darkness, beyond the crater. 'Sounds like we might be in for a spot of subsidence, thanks to you, Doctor.'

'Etta!' said the Doctor delightedly. 'In the nick of time, as always.'

Tony shone his torch into Etta's face.

'Do you mind?' she said, raising a hand.

'Sorry,' he said, and lowered the beam, lighting the way ahead for her.

'My, what a big hole,' she said. 'My garden fence is down there somewhere. Mind you, I think I prefer it without the tree. Much more neighbourly, don't you think?'

'Er… yes,' said Tony.

Etta was carrying a large plate, which she held out towards the group. 'Who's for a Halloween cookie?'

The cookies were in the shape of bats, coated with black icing, with red dots for eyes.

'I think I'll pass if you don't mind,' Martha said with a shudder.

'Me too,' said Rick, then caught a warning look from his parents. 'Then again, maybe not.'

'Lovely,' said the Doctor, shoving most of a cookie into his mouth. He made exaggerated yum-yum noises, and grabbed another from the plate, then, after a moment's hesitation, a third, which he dropped into his pocket.

'Right,' he said, 'well, better go. Things to do, people to see. Goodbye all. Come on, Martha.'

Without waiting for a reply, he turned and strode away, leaving Martha smiling sheepishly round at the group.

'Sorry,' she said. 'He doesn't like goodbyes. Well, I'd better...' She wafted a hand vaguely in the Doctor's direction.

Etta smiled. 'Go on, dear. You catch up with your spaceman. And tell him... thank you. On behalf of us all. Tell him thank you for saving our town.'

'I will,' said Martha, and raised a hand. 'Well, bye everyone. Maybe I'll see you again some time.'

She doubted she would, though. That was what life with the Doctor was like. Meet people, share extraordinary times, move on.

'Wait up, Doctor,' she shouted, jogging after his gangly silhouette. And although she wanted to, she didn't look back.

Not once.

Acknowledgements

Many thanks to Justin for opening the door, to Paul and Mark for sharing the adventure, to Gary for the guided tour, to Russell and the gang for giving us the programme we always dreamed of, and to Mike Tucker, Graham Groom, Gareth Preston and Alan Richardson for feeding the geek.

Also available from BBC Books
featuring the Doctor and Rose
as played by Christopher Eccleston and Billie Piper:

DOCTOR · WHO

THE CLOCKWISE MAN
by Justin Richards

THE MONSTERS INSIDE
by Stephen Cole

WINNER TAKES ALL
by Jacqueline Rayner

THE DEVIANT STRAIN
by Justin Richards

ONLY HUMAN
by Gareth Roberts

THE STEALERS OF DREAMS
by Steve Lyons

DOCTOR·WHO

Sting of the Zygons
by Stephen Cole

ISBN 978 1 84607 225 3
UK £6.99 US $11.99/$14.99 CDN

The TARDIS lands the Doctor and Martha in the
Lake District in 1909, where a small village has been
terrorised by a giant, scaly monster. The search is on
for the elusive 'Beast of Westmorland', and explorers,
naturalists and hunters from across the country are
descending on the fells. King Edward VII himself is
on his way to join the search, with a knighthood for
whoever finds the Beast.

But there is a more sinister presence at work in the
Lakes than a mere monster on the rampage, and the
Doctor is soon embroiled in the plans of an old and
terrifying enemy. As the hunters become the hunted, a
desperate battle of wits begins – with the future of the
entire world at stake…

The Last Dodo

by Jacqueline Rayner

ISBN 978 1 84607 224 6

UK £6.99 US $11.99/$14.99 CDN

The Doctor and Martha go in search of a real live dodo, and are transported by the TARDIS to the mysterious Museum of the Last Ones. There, in the Earth section, they discover every extinct creature up to the present day, all still alive and in suspended animation.

Preservation is the museum's only job – collecting the last of every endangered species from all over the universe. But exhibits are going missing…

Can the Doctor solve the mystery before the museum's curator adds the last of the Time Lords to her collection?

DOCTOR·WHO

Wooden Heart

by Martin Day

ISBN 978 1 84607 226 0

UK £6.99 US $11.99/$14.99 CDN

A vast starship, seemingly deserted and spinning slowly in the void of deep space. Martha and the Doctor explore this drifting tomb, and discover that they may not be alone after all…

Who survived the disaster that overcame the rest of the crew? What continues to power the vessel? And why has a stretch of wooded countryside suddenly appeared in the middle of the craft?

As the Doctor and Martha journey through the forest, they find a mysterious, fogbound village – a village traumatised by missing children and prophecies of its own destruction.

DOCTOR·WHO

Sick Building

by Paul Magrs

ISBN 978 1 84607 269 7

UK £6.99 US $11.99/$14.99 CDN

Tiermann's World: a planet covered in wintry woods and roamed by sabre-toothed tigers and other savage beasts. The Doctor is here to warn Professor Tiermann, his wife and their son that a terrible danger is on its way.

The Tiermanns live in luxury, in a fantastic, futuristic, fully automated Dreamhome, under an impenetrable force shield. But that won't protect them from the Voracious Craw. A gigantic and extremely hungry alien creature is heading remorselessly towards their home. When it gets there everything will be devoured.

Can they get away in time? With the force shield cracking up, and the Dreamhome itself deciding who should or should not leave, things are looking desperate…

DOCTOR·WHO

Wetworld

by Mark Michalowski

ISBN 978 1 84607 271 0

UK £6.99 US $11.99/$14.99 CDN

When the TARDIS makes a disastrous landing in the swamps of the planet Sunday, the Doctor has no choice but to abandon Martha and try to find help. But the tranquillity of Sunday's swamps is deceptive, and even the TARDIS can't protect Martha forever.

The human pioneers of Sunday have their own dangers to face: homeless and alone, they're only just starting to realise that Sunday's wildlife isn't as harmless as it first seems. Why are the native otters behaving so strangely, and what is the creature in the swamps that is so interested in the humans, and the new arrivals?

The Doctor and Martha must fight to ensure that human intelligence doesn't become the greatest danger of all.

Coming soon from BBC Books
featuring the Doctor and Martha
as played by David Tennant and Freema Agyeman:

DOCTOR · WHO

WISHING WELL
by Trevor Baxendale

THE PIRATE LOOP
by Simon Guerrier

PEACEMAKER
by James Swallow

DOCTOR·WHO
The Inside Story
by Gary Russell
ISBN 978 0 56348 649 7
£14.99

In March 2005, a 900-year-old alien in a police public call box made a triumphant return to our television screens. *The Inside Story* takes us behind the scenes to find out how the series was commissioned, made and brought into the twenty-first century. Gary Russell has talked extensively to everyone involved in the show, from the Tenth Doctor himself, David Tennant, and executive producer Russell T Davies, to the people normally hidden inside monster suits or behind cameras. Everyone has an interesting story to tell.

The result is the definitive account of how the new *Doctor Who* was created. With exclusive access to design drawings, backstage photographs, costume designs and other previously unpublished pictures, *The Inside Story* covers the making of all twenty-six episodes of Series One and Two, plus the Christmas specials, as well as an exclusive look ahead to the third series.

Also available from BBC Books:

DOCTOR·WHO

Creatures and Demons
by *Justin Richards*
ISBN 978 1 84607 229 1
UK £7.99 US $12.99/$15.99 CDN

Throughout his many adventures in time and space, the Doctor has encountered aliens, monsters, creatures and demons from right across the universe. In this third volume of alien monstrosities and dastardly villains, *Doctor Who* expert and acclaimed author Justin Richards describes some of the evils the Doctor has fought in over forty years of time travel.

From the grotesque Abzorbaloff to the monstrous Empress of the Racnoss, from giant maggots to the Daleks of the secret Cult of Skaro, from the Destroyer of Worlds to the ancient Beast itself… This book brings together more of the terrifying enemies the Doctor has battled against.

Illustrated throughout with stunning photographs and design drawings from the current series of *Doctor Who* and his previous 'classic' incarnations, this book is a treat for friends of the Doctor whatever their age, and whatever planet they come from…